The
Tomato Can

The Tomato Can

A novel by

RON ROSS

OYSTER BAY BOOKS, *Publisher*

Published by Oyster Bay Books
Oyster Bay, New York

DEDICATION

I had a friend who was the best optometrist there ever was because he enabled me to see humor and sensitivity where others perceived only the sinister and harshness.

Doctor Marvin Goldberg was to the World of Boxing what Father Flanagan was to Boys Town. In Doc's mind, there was no such thing as a bad prizefighter. The courage and bravery required to climb those four steps into the ring more than compensated for any misdeeds that might be committed by one of these young warriors. He was truly an enigma. No gentler nor more considerate human being graced the streets of New York and yet he loved uncondi-tionally the most violent and primitive of sports with a passion and devotion beyond reason and intellect. It was through my twenty-five year friendship and association with Doc, wherein he refueled and reawakened my interest in a sport that I participated in as a young man, that much of the situations and characters in this book are gleaned.

Doc served the sport in every capacity from boxing judge, matchmaker, ring announcer at Madison Square Garden (as well as all the smaller fight clubs in New York and major arenas throughout the country), manager, hosted his own radio sports show, wrote a newspaper boxing column and in 1991 was appointed President of the Boxing Officials Association of New York. All of this was in addition to his full time profession as an optometrist.

In Doc's world, there was no room for "tomato cans," stumble bums or fixed fights. He had that rare, innate ability to cut through seaminess and tawdriness with a keen understanding and appreciation of the human spirit bolstered and enhanced by a dry, twinkle-eyed sense of humor. Every fighter that came before him was accorded the respect of a world champion and anyone connected with the sport could always rely on Doc Goldberg for a favor or a helping hand. The endless hours that he devoted to the sport could never be equated in dollars or personal gain of any sort for his was a labor strictly of love. He did not prosper from the sport, rather, the sport prospered from him.

When Doctor Marvin Goldberg passed away on Christmas Day, 1992, they tolled the ten-count in his honor from the ring at Madison Square Garden. The boxing world lost not just a great friend but one of the few people who put into the game without ever thinking of taking out. No dedication or memorial can adequately honor the person that he was. I simply want to say "Thank you Marvin for a great and fulfilling friendship."

Ron Ross

The Tomato Can

ROUND 1

I guess Friday nights were always my favorite night. No...I don't guess...I KNOW Friday nights are my favorite nights. First, I dress up. Not too much, but just enough to feel good about myself. A white shirt, open at the collar, no tie—maybe when it's cold, a turtle neck; a sport jacket and patent leather shoes—a good fifty-cent Havana cigar in the jacket pocket, and now I begin feelin' like a million bucks. Then I get a ride with a couple of the boys or else I grab a cab to take me uptown to the Garden. Every Friday night is fight night at the Garden, except when the circus or somethin' special like that comes to town and then Friday night gets pushed a little further uptown to St. Nick's. A lot of the same crowd, but it's different. It's missin' class, both in the crowd an' the fighters. I'm not sayin' you don't get some good scraps, you do; but the big boys, the guys who get purses with three zeros at the end— they're for the Garden. They sleep when the circus is in town. And that lobby on Eighth Avenue between 49th and 50th...forget it, baby, that's my world.

A lot of the guys like the ponies. They're there every day—Aqueduct, Belmont; when the weather gets cold, Hey! they say, Hialeah's only a suitcase and a train ride away. But, me, gimme my Friday nights at the Garden. I get there like a half hour before the opening four-rounder. All the big guys 'n the heavy hitters know me 'n there's a lot of hellos an' backslappin'. Big Nose Sallie always has my ticket waitin' for me with the guy at the Advance Sale window. We talk, we bullshit, an' on the good nights one of the boys will q.t. me on who's in the bag that night. Hey, paisan, that's where I get the bread to put on my table. Now remember, it's not a regular thing, it's not an all the time thing—an' there are certain specials that are reserved only for the Big Boys. . .even I don't get a sniff of those. But I get enough to keep me very happy, and in enough pasta to have me goin' to Tony to always let out the pants waist another little bit. . .just a little, not a lot. I don't ever wanna get sloppy fat. One in the family is enough.

But that's not why I love my Friday nights at the Garden. It don't hurt, but it ain't the reason. I just love it. Plain an' simple. There ain't no reason—it's just a whole feeling, you know, good friends, good times, that's what it's all about. And then after the fights I walk the two blocks to Angelina's, on Ninth Avenue and forty-eighth Street. If you told me my mother, God bless her, was in the kitchen doing the cooking, I would almost believe it. There's only a few restaurants, outside of steak houses, where I can walk in and enjoy the food. Once you take me away from Mulberry and Grand or Coney Island, that only leaves Angelina's. And that's why I don't wear a tie on Friday nights, besides the fact that it squeezes the pits out of my adam's apple. Usually, the spaghetti sauce just misses my shirt, but it never, never misses my tie. So, at 11:30, 12 o'clock any Friday night I'm eatin' pasta fazoo, spaghetti with Angelina's red clam sauce, a bottle of chianti and finish it off with a big piece of rum cake; I can drink the rum cake—I swear to God, I can drink it! Then I light up my stogie, which I cannot do at home without the old lady chasin' me into the toilet with it; there's no squawkin' brats at Angelina's an' there's no smelly, leakin' garbage bags to take out while I freeze my collones. I think you're beginnin' to get the idea why I love Friday night so much, huh?

Anyhow, on this one particular Friday night I walk out of the Garden so nauseous from the stink I just saw, I think, maybe I shouldn't go to Angelina's in case I am unable to hold down my food. But this is a very drastic solution which I soon squelch. Why make it a double punishment? It is enough that I wasn't cut in on what I'm sure was a very big kitty. No need to deprive myself any further. Also, I am with this doll Mitzi, who I socialize with on many of my Friday nights. Although I do not make plans to meet her, which I know would be like cheating, she is very often at the Garden, and it is like taken for granted that when she is at the Garden, she is my lady friend. I do not even know how she gets into the Garden, except I'm pretty sure it has a lot to do with the fact that she, too, is a friend of Big Nose Sallie. Ya see, Mitzi is from the neighborhood but there is absolutely no socializing with her in the neighborhood because the old lady, without a question would pull out her hair and maybe even kill her. When we first got married there was a little talk over the clotheslines on our block, and my wife bumps into Mitzi in the butcher shop – now, I wasn't there, but they told me that if Giuseppe, the butcher, and his helper didn't get the meat cleaver out of my old lady's hands, there would be no more Mitzi. I had to give my old lady a couple of pot shots that night for givin' me a bad name in the neighborhood. I learned then that she takes a good punch – an' that's before she put on the heft. I also learned then that she gives a pretty good shot. . .and she fights dirty. What I mean is I don't want any rematches so I don't cheat anymore – I never go out or socialize in my own neighborhood.

Luigi, who is Angelina's husband and takes care of the whole front part of the restaurant, shakes my hand and takes me and Mitzi to my table, which is large enough for six people because usually I get company to join us. I don't get the bear-hug and then the backwards, bowing tiptoe to the table from Luigi; that's reserved for the "Dwarf" Langella, Big Nose Sallie an' guys like that. Meanwhile I am always wondering how a guy like Luigi with a wife like Angelina always looks like a ballet dancer. He gotta keep puttin' his finger down his t'roat – I'm sure that's the answer.

We just start eatin' a small order of scungili when Joey the Clown walks over and says, "What a smelleroo!" I lift a fork of the wiggly stuff to my nose to take a sniff even though I think it is a very impolite thing for the Clown to say when two people are dinin'. Then I realize he is not referring to what is on the table, but what we saw at the Garden.

First, I gotta explain somethin'. The Clown is not the Clown because he is a funny person, which I promise you he is not, or because he wears funny clothes or has a funny face – well, as far as his clothes, sometimes maybe and if you think a face that makes a cat look like a porcupine is funny, okay, I'll back off on that, too. But that is still not why he is called the Clown. In my neighborhood, which is Coney Island, almost every body gets a name, that is, besides the name he gets from his family and the church. You get a name and that's who you are, forever. The Clown happened to be born with the monicker, Joseph DiCollonna. So, not too long after he got rid of his diapers he became Joey the Clown.

I wave my fork, which sends some scungili flying, for Joey and his steady girl, Goldie, to sit down at our table. Whenever I look at Goldie I think Joey had to win her at a penny arcade. She is a kewpie doll combination of Betty Boop and Sheena, Queen of the Jungle. I think even Joey's old lady gotta be proud that he has such a side-dish. Except if you were to shake her I'm sure you would hear little pebbles rattling around in the belfry. He is very shocked and perturbed at the evening's events, probably more so because he was not invited to share in the golden goose party, which I notice only built up his appetite when as soon as he sits down he somehow has a fork in his hand and is without invitation becoming a partner in our scungili. I offer to order another dish of scungili. I really do this to embarrass the Clown, not to stuff his face or his belly but this is completely beyond him and he wipes his mouth with the back of his hand and says, "No, this is fine. Would ya believe that bum LaMotta?" He is referring, of course, to what transpired at the Garden that night right in front of our eyes. For what our eyes told us we might as well have been selling pencils on Broadway. "I always tell ya," pipes up Goldie, "if you can't say something nice about someone, don't say anything at all. Anyhow, you never know who might be sittin' at the next table."

I can truly understand why sometimes the Clown gets exasperated. "Shut up, Goldie," he pleads like a real gentleman, although I have the feeling at that moment that Goldie is one word away from making an appointment with her orthodontist. But the main reason for the Clown being in such a bad mood is not just

realizing that Jake LaMotta will never win the Academy
Award, but that he can't even act as good as the big
monkey, King Kong, who at least knew how to fall down
from the top of the Empire State Building while
LaMotta couldn't even fall down inside of three strands
of rope to the canvas in Madison Square Garden. "I
mean," Joey continued, "if a guy's doin' business, let him
do business. Dat bum was insultin' our intelligence,
Sonny."

I thought for a second and answered, "Well,
sometimes a guy's gotta do what he's gotta do, even if
he really don't wanna do it." Goldie's eyes widened,
"What'd he say, Joey? I don't understand what he said."
Joey ignored her because I don't think he understood,
either. To tell you the truth, I don't think I understood
what I just said!

"Hey, Sonny, tell me," Joey looked me square in the
eye, "were you feeding on this one? You sonuvagun, you
had the line, didn't you?" I told him the truth, and that
was "No". I guess my answer about what "a guy's gotta
do" made him feel that way. I suppose I said that because
I always liked LaMotta. I always thought of him as one
of the boys, even though he came from the Bronx, which
you couldn't really hold against him as he had no choice
about where to be born. With me, if your name ended
with an 'O' or it was split in half with two capitals,
already you couldn't be all bad. And if you weren't all
bad, that was the first step to bein' a good guy.

On the night of this stink bomb, LaMotta, who was one of the very best middleweights around, stepped up in weight class to fight this new whiz from Philly—a colored kid called Blackjack Billy Fox who they were building up for a shot at the light heavyweight championship. He knocked out everyone he fought. But when you see him fight you think that list includes his grandmother, your grandmother, my grandmother but not Aunt Matilda because that would be takin' too much of a chance. He throws punches like he's in a fight in the girls' locker room. You know the guy hadda been fed a steady diet of tomato cans. On the other hand, LaMotta is a guy who c'n chop down an oak tree without a hatchet. He zeros in on the body an' breaks you in half. Everybody who knows anything about the fight game says this should be no fight at all and Billy Fox should be out shoppin' for a new belly button. Only what happens is every time LaMotta hits the kid he has to hold him up to keep him from fallin' down. This can get pretty tirin' so he stops hittin' the kid an' in the fourth round LaMotta, in front of twenty thousand people sits down on the bottom strand of rope—it looks like he's walkin' a tightrope on his ass—an' the kid is powder-puffin' him like your sister would do if you hung her bloomers out the front window. You see, LaMotta never got knocked off his feet in his life, an' that's where the real stink comes in. It don't take Mr. I.Q. to know now that Jake is in the tank. The only thing is, whoever picked up the tab got short changed by about twenty-four inches, which is by how much Jake's ass misses the canvas. LaMotta was willin' to go in the tank, because in return he's promised a title shot, which he gets. But he cannot ruin his record of never bein' knocked off his feet. For that he got too much pride. This whole thing makes such a smell in the Garden that the guys up in the balcony who have very sensitive nostrils, they start throwin' everything they can get their hands on into the ring, like beer bottles, peanuts, newspapers. It's sorta like a sacrifice to the gods, hopin' maybe they'll get rid of the smell, or at least whoever made the smell.

Now Vito Fusillo has come over and is sitting at my table and he, too, is grumblin' about that bum LaMotta who was a traitor to all his friends and fans. Vito, who is one of the neighborhood guys who made good in very big style, he owns the Villa Vito in Bay Ridge, is really a horse player. The Fuse, which everyone calls him, is not a real finesse person when it comes to the ins and outs of boxing. I am in the middle of explaining to everyone what I really think they saw, "So the real problem is LaMotta is too much fighter. He is not a tomato can...." when Goldie cuts in with as much class as a Bowery bum clearing his left nostril, "What's all this shit about a tomato can? What are we talkin' about—a prize fight or a grocery store?"

"Excuse me, will Princess Elizabeth please repeat that question!" She was really beginning to irritate me now, which is a strange feeling for me to have with a broad that is constructed like Goldie. "It is Princess Elizabeth, isn't it? Who else could have such proper upbringing?"

"Hey, come on, Sonny," the Clown grunted, "I'm the one who takes care of my woman. Show a little respect, will ya?"

"I'm showin' as little respect as possible, Joey." I smiled as I said that. You can call the Clown any name under the sun...you can probably even stick pins in him as long as you smile. The Clown likes smiles. The Clown turns to Goldie, "What'd I tell ya about talkin' nice, especially to my friends?" Goldie puts on this do-me-something face and says, "I always talk nice to everybody. Your problem is, you don't know what nice is!" I am now thinking what a waste it would be to see Goldie splattered on Angelina's wall like a mural. The Bay of Naples or Vesuvius belongs there, not Goldie; so I quickly do my best to make sure that Angelina's decor does not change, "We are not talking about a grocery store tomato can, Goldie. We are talkin' about another kind of tomato can, at least one of which some of us at this table are personally acquainted with."

"I was once pretty well acquainted with some tub of lard," Goldie chirps, "but I really don't believe I ever had the pleasure of knowing a tomato can. I hope that does not make me a bad person."

This Goldie is a real card, maybe even an overstacked deck, to whom I reply, "Not being a neighborhood person, Goldie, you happen to be the one person present who could not know Tommy 'Tomato Can' Curcio." At which Mitzi, the Clown and Vito, just like they were the Andrew Sisters or the Inkspots, all say together, "Tommy Curcio? The Cockie Doodie Boy?"

"Hey, let's show a little gratitude. The kid helped make abodonza for all of us", I reminded them.

"Yeah, and we almost give it all back because of him", says the Clown, still pickin' away at my food. "That's why the Dwarf probably gets him a new pair of shoes— made outta concrete!"

"A lot was happening then which you probably don't even know about. He was a good guy...he was loyal and he had respect for everyone."

Vito cut in, "He was a screw-up. He mighta been a good kid but he was a big-time screw-up!"

Goldie now gives out this big sigh and with a real exasperated look says, "I still don't know what a tomato can is when it's not in a grocery store; all I know is Jake LaMotta, who got his ass kicked tonight, really didn't get his ass kicked and is not a tomato can while Tommy something-or-other, who isn't even here tonight, is a tomato can. Am I possibly sitting with the guest panel from 'It Pays To Be Ignorant?' " Now I am having second thoughts as to maybe Goldie should be a mural in Angelina's. In fact, if the Clown is still of such inclination, I would probably volunteer part of the labor involved in creating such a work of art. But at this moment the Clown is otherwise disposed. It seems that the waiter removed the empty platters of scungilli – the Clown made certain they were completely empty, – and replaced them with my next course, a heaping bowl of linguini with white clam sauce which the Clown was industriously sopping up with a dripping hunk of bread. My linguini, thus far, was not violated but I realized it was in imminent danger as I very, very inconspic- uously started sliding my dish towards me and hopefully, out of the reach of the Clown, whose hand with the bread kept following the dish like it had a magnet. I knew then that Goldie would survive while my linguini might not.

While the rest of me was busily occupied in defending my Friday night pasta, my mouth was doing its best without the use of my brain, which was also on linguini reconnaissance, to give Goldie a definition of "tomato can" because no way was she going to find it in any dictionary by Noah Webster whose name is one of the endearing things that has followed me from my one and only year at Abraham Lincoln High School. "You see, Goldie, there are prize fighters, there are palookas, there are stumble bums and there are tomato cans. A palooka is a guy whose head ya c'n bang from today till tomorrow, but it's so empty inside that there's nothin' much to scramble and his chin is usually made from cast iron and he hits back sometimes with two concrete hands. He is not too much fun to fight even though he is going no place because his brain is slower than a sleeping snail. A stumble bum is a guy who got nothin' but needs some booze or coffee change and is willing to get all crunched up and slid under a door to get it. You c'n usually recognize him by his nose which sometimes touches his ear-lobe and his round heels, which he rocks on. But a tomato can—a tomato can is somethin' else again. He is somewhere between good 'n lousy. He ain't got a chance to get to the top even with an elevator. He's a guy whose hands are just a little too slow, not enough snap in his punch, a little too much tinkly stuff in his chin and as far as that little extra something it takes to be a champion—he couldn't even buy it at a fire sale at Gimbel's or Macy's. But he's just good enough to climb in there with the guys on the way up, and a good tomato can is like an artist. The managers and promoters love him, because he's the guy they can call at any time to go in with one of their kids who's a comer. A tomato can does not give you agita. He goes in there, puts on a show—and loses. A good tomato can loses beautifully. Tommy Curcio was as good a tomato can as there ever was."

"That was all very educational, Sonny," comes back Goldie, "but why a tomato can? Why can't such a person be called, say, a box of doughnuts or a roll of toilet paper?" I could not believe this broad; her mouth gotta run on a motor! "It don't matter, Goldie. It is just a figure of speech." I am now a college professor. "Like, if you put a tomato can in a ring it wouldn't worry you at all – it would just stand there 'n you c'n hit it and it wouldn't hit you back."

"And a roll of toilet paper would hit you back?" There was no quit in her at all.

"Whatsa matter wit' ya, Goldie?" The Clown was coming to my rescue now, which is like savin' a drownin' man by throwing him an anchor. "It ain't up to you or me or Sonny what words to use – God makes language."

All of us turn slowly and look at the Clown because we do not believe what we just heard but naturally, only Goldie's mouth is able to work, "God makes language? You mean God decided to call your friend Tommy a tomato can instead of a roll of toilet paper?"

"Yeah, sort of. God makes language, God makes words, God makes everything. You don't think words just happen, do ya? God makes 'em, ain't that right, Vito?", the Clown no longer looked so sure of himself, but Vito, with a stroke of diplomatic genius says, "I think we should keep religion out of this."

Just then "Dwarf" Langella and Big Nose Sallie walk in. They nod politely to us but do not stop to say anything like even 'Hello' but go straight to their table in the back, led there by Luigi, who is now doing his backwards ballet dance which is filled with bows and curtsies. There is this cat-ate-the-canary kind of smile

on Big Nose Sallie's face (the Dwarf's face, which is like
old leather, is too stiff for his lips to move up or down);
this smile was a sure sign that Sallie and the Dwarf
were invited to LaMotta's pool Party. That they did not
invite their goombahs to the party does not mean that
they are selfish. It just shows that they know how to
keep their mouths closed when they are asked to—a
quality that does not go unrewarded in our society.

ROUND 2

No business is ever done in this town without Donato Langella being in on the ground floor. There are numerous reasons for this, among which, he has paid his dues over many years; he has much smarts; he is one very tough individual and he is a very large person —so large that wherever he goes people stare at him in astonishment without even meaning to. He is a smidgen over six feet seven inches tall and although I, personally, have never put him on a scale I can pretty safely say there are almost three hundred pounds of him, none of which is belly-bulge or baby fat. Looking at the "Dwarf" is like seeing this big oak tree that someone who is not a very good carpenter went at with a hammer and a chisel and with just a coupla strokes here and there chopped out a nose, two big ears, eyes and a one-stroke mouth and then did not bother using any sandpaper at all. The black top-coat and black slouch hat that he always wore further detracted from the warmth and friendliness that we knew was buried somewhere deep within (and with such an abundance of size it could be very deep, indeed).

Donato, as a young man, but of the same size and disposition as today's Donato, had this little chore of collecting delinquent payments of loans to local businessmen and shopkeepers. This was our equivalent to starting as a stockroom boy in other areas of the business sector. On this particular occasion he is engaged in a business discussion with the new owner of the corner candy store who has just learned from young Langella of a small weekly payment that he has never previously been informed of and he is, to say the least, just a trifle reluctant. Never one to waste time, Donato Langella tells the angry, young storeowner that they will now play basketball, which, probably because of his size, is one of his favorite games. Mr. Store-owner points out that there are only two people, to which Langella explains that is fine. That is the perfect number for this game – one player and one basketball. Donato, of course, will be the player and the person left over will be the basketball. He further describes how he, at times will dribble or bounce this basketball all over the floor and at other times how he will throw the basketball into the air, hoping to score two points. The candy store man does not seem to think that he will enjoy this game as much as Langella will, so, instead, he unhappily hands over the money to him and looking way up into his eyes, sputters in frustration, "You wouldn't be so… so…tough if you were a…a…dwarf!" Everyone in earshot, including Donato, agreed that made a lot of sense. So, to this day, although no one ever says it to his face, he is the Dwarf. We know that he knows and we even think he likes it but because the Dwarf does not know how to smile we cannot be absolutely certain.

Without sayin' a single word, which in itself is a minor miracle, Goldie pops up and walks across the restaurant towards the Dwarf's table with every eye in the place followin' this swishin' round bottom wrapped in a tight-fittin' red sarong-like dress—every eye, that is, except the Clown's, whose eyes, it seems, is searching the floor by his feet like he is looking for this hole where he can climb in an' bury himself.

"Good evening, Sallie, good evening, Mr. Langella, would you gentlemen care to join us at our table?"

The Dwarf does not have to look up at her although she is standing and he is sitting. "No, thank you, Goldie, I have this headache and I think it would be better if I were away from people and noise tonight."

"Oh, I am so sorry to hear that. I presume that you gentlemen were at the prize fights tonight?" When there was no response Goldie continued undaunted, "My gentleman friend Joey, and also Vito and Sonny say what they saw was that Jake LaMotta did not do his utmost to prevail in tonight's boxing match and this disturbs them greatly because they invested their hard-earned money out of loyalty and also based on their belief that he was an honorable person."

Big Nose Sallie gives with this broad, know-it-all

smile an' says, "They gotta believe what they see, 'specially if they got good eye-sight. What'd you see, Goldie?"

Goldie shrugs, gives a little wriggle an' bats her eyelashes, "I guess a girl sees things different than a guy. I saw LaMotta get beat up, but that don't mean a thing because it's like when we go to the movies – at the parts where I always cry, Joey is always laughin'– I mean laughin' real loud."

The Dwarf is now looking at her like she is some very strange person. "You know, Goldie," he says, "when I go to the track there's eight – nine – ten horses out there. I got a one in about ten chance. Here at the fights you just got two pugs – a fifty-fifty chance. What could be more fair? Goldie, I think maybe they're sore-losers, huh?"

Goldie leans closer and in her most confidential voice, whispers, "I think that what really bothers them is they are insulted that Jake LaMotta was not at all professional. They said that he is a very good prize fighter but he is not a good Tomato Can like Tommy Curcio was."

Now I gotta admit – this was an attention-getter. The Dwarf's face turns dark like a rain cloud an' his eyes bulge from their sockets like two cannon balls. This gotta hurt the Dwarf's face because it hardly ever moves at all; Big Nose Sallie's adam's apple is movin' around like there's a ping-pong game goin' on in his t'roat; Vito's eyes are turned up, lookin' at the ceiling, just like the guy in the elevator who did a no-no; an' the Clown, I think he's busy lookin' for a shovel so he c'n really bury himself now. As for me, I am at this time very seriously thinkin' of that mural on Angelina's wall.

Disregarding the "dumb blonde" label, and Goldie is as blonde as a bottle of peroxide can make a person, one begins to wonder—just how dumb or how smart is this broad? Obviously, she is smart enough to get out of a place where lightning is about to strike. Her high heel spikes make a clickety-click on the floor as she sashays back to our table like a bunny rabbit who just filched the farmer's prize carrot and announces this profound discovery, "I don't think those two like talkin' about your Tomato Can friend!"

Mitzi, who has been very quiet through this whole meal, mostly because I think she is hypnotized watching the Clown devour our entire dinner, now decides to add her two cents, "You are right, Goldie, it is a most uncomfortable topic of conversation for them. In fact, it is a forbidden topic of conversation."

"No kidding!" Goldie is wide-eyed now. "But you guys don't seem to have any trouble talkin' about him."

"You're right," Mitzi answers, "it's really just the Dwarf and Big Nose Sallie that find it a very sensitive subject. Why don't you explain it, Sonny? She's from Joisey. She don't know nothin.' "

This I need about as much as the Clown needs a
menu. "Vito," I am hoping to pass this off to someone
other than myself, "You are older and more familiar with
the situation than I am. I think it would be better
coming from you."

"Sonny, you are quite the bullshit artist, but you are
trying to con a con man. The truth is, I carry around
a very large burden of guilt over this, which although
I keep it inside of myself, I do not enjoy talking about it."

"You said it yourself, Vito," the Clown reminds him,
"Tommy was a screw-up. You shouldn't oughta feel
guilty—you was good to him."

"Yeah, but I sometimes wonder how things woulda
been if...you know...if he was just Tommy
Curcio...and...aah, you know what I mean."

"Go on, Sonny," says Mitzi, "your mouth hasn't had
any exercise tonight anyhow," a very tactful reference
to the meal I did not eat, "so explain to Goldie before
she busts out of her girdle."

"I do not wear a girdle, Sweetie-Pie," Goldie protests
with this horrific look on her face. Thanks to Jake
LaMotta, I see there is no getting out of this one. So
I lean back in my chair, take a good stretch and realize
it is time to remove from my jacket pocket where it
has resided patiently all night, my faithful Havana and
light it up. My only regret is that on this particular night
I cannot call it my after-dinner smoke which is what
it was intended to be, but you know what is said about

"the best laid plans of mice and men"– in fact, included in my educational background is this little tidbit that the guy who said that, Robert Burns, grew up to be a cigar himself.

I go on to explain the best I can about Tommy Curcio, who was my friend and who was a good guy who just did not get all the breaks. It is not too easy to tell everything to Goldie because there are things we do not discuss much outside of our own place, and these things are important to what I am relating. It is now 1947, which is a pretty good time in most of our lives but this whole thing with Tommy goes back to the early days of the Depression, just about when Roosevelt first gets elected President and Tommy was in the 8th grade at P.S. 188 in Coney Island. I was a few years older'n Tommy and was just becomin' a regular at the Mermaid Social-Athletic Club, which, although it did not give out any sheepskin diplomas, did offer what I believed was the education I was lookin' for. It took me a whole year at Lincoln High School to realize the thing I liked the best was going to the football games and gettin' into fights with the kids from the other schools when they started singin' "Stinkin' Lincoln." Even then the seeds of loyalty and honor were firmly implanted in my breast. (You think Vito was right what he said about me?)

ROUND 3

I hadda pass the Mermaid S.A.C. every day goin' to and comin' from school and I could not believe there were people that lived the way these guys did. It looked like they hardly ever got their hands dirty; they were always hangin' aroun', laughin', talkin' playin' cards, shootin' pool an' they even had a bocci court in the backyard. Some of the older guys would sit around all day an' play this game called moo'da where they would bang their hands on the table, then throw out a hand with a certain number of fingers and call out at the same time the number in Italian that the fingers of both players would have. It was too fast an' crazy a game for me ever to learn. They had their own bar and their own espresso machine. All this was very impressive to me who came from a family whose old man would be out at the crack of dawn each morning for a shapeup on the docks, or sometimes he'd work in a marble place in Bath Beach, then instead of comin' home he'd go straight to his night job as a counterman at Feltman's on Surf Avenue, from where on occasion he'd bring home some left-over hot dogs which my mother would chop up and put in her lasagna. If you have never tasted hot dog lasagna—don't worry about it too much. My old man did not have the time or the energy to laugh or talk or play any games. The few times that I was still awake when he got home I would see him stagger in from exhaustion and without a single word flop into the one easy chair that we had in the little alcove we called a living room. He had this unbelievable ability to have his whole body up to his neck sink into the chair, immediately be sound asleep, but his head would never touch the back of the chair which was covered by a doily—it would bob around, snoring, always staying about an inch away from the doily, like it knew, God forbid it should make contact—Whammo! Electrocution or worse. His head was trained good; just like those Russian dogs (somethin' else I learned at Lincoln), only this time my mother was the scientist. Whenever he used to come home and fall into his easy chair, my mother would run in shouting, "You getta you head from that chair with that-a greasy hair!"

And he would grumble back, but knowing he was whipped, "What'sa da napkin for?"

"The doily's-a for company and to keepa the chair clean—it's-a not for your head!"

I would never stop marveling how he would be able to sleep while his head hung out by itself. But, in spite of the doily taboo, according to my mother, my old man was the model by which all men were measured. If you didn't finish your day totally wiped out, dirty, sweaty and bent over, then you hadda be a bum. In other words she did not share my admiration or esteem for the guys from the Mermaid Social Athletic Club.

Even though I really didn't know my old man because I hardly ever saw him, I loved him. He was my father and I loved him like a son loves a father, but I did not want to grow up to be like him. Now, the guys at the Club – they learned what it was all about somehow and if I could learn from them, I knew it would make me very happy. I didn't have no old man, no uncle or no relative of any kind that hung out there. If I did it wouldn't be any big deal gettin' in an' bein' one of the crowd. For someone like me, you start hangin' aroun' and not wisin' off. You run little errands for the guys like pickin' up cigarettes for them at the candy store, or coffee, newspapers – whatever they might need. You pick up a broom without bein' asked an' sweep up the sidewalk in front of the Club. It becomes natural when you hang around and keep your nose clean that when you get a little older, one day the guys call you in and let you do something like work behind the bar or empty out the ashtrays. Eventually you find yourself sittin' in the poker games or shootin' pool; once in a while you'll be doin' little jobs for the Dwarf or Big Nose Sallie like deliverin' a package to someone, goin' to the track an' placin' their bets for them when they cannot go themselves, selling raffle books an' chances, goin' aroun' with punchboards—you would never believe what a nice piece of change we make from this stuff. An' for the guys that don't mind punching clocks and doin' real work, the Dwarf is very well connected—he is like a one-man employment agency. But the icing on the cake is all the little inside tips we are fed. There is much less left to chance in this world than most people would believe.

The Club is not a place with a regular routine where ya gotta do this or ya gotta do that. It is a friendly, casual place where you horse around or relax or do whatever ya wanna do, but everyone there knows one thing—you always show respect and listen to the Dwarf or to his Number One man, Big Nose Sallie. The Dwarf does not do too much talking or socializing. He is very big on grunting and eye-talking. Your voice can do a lot of resting when you have eyes that move around like the Dwarf's and can direct you just by the way they look at you. But no one doubts that the man has brains to match his size. He has proven it many times in the past. When there are messages to go out or things to be done, you generally hear about it from Big Nose Sallie, who also is nobody's dumbbell and is much more around the guys than the Dwarf. Salvatore Pignasale does not have a nose that would win any kind of a medal in a big nose contest. On the other hand, neither would he win anything in a little nose contest. So let us say that his nose was inconsequential to say the least but

Big Nose Sallie has a much nicer ring to it than Mr. Pignasale.

All of this is too personal for me to talk about, especially to someone like Goldie, who I gotta consider to be an outsider. Also it is not very manly to talk about such stuff. Anyhow, the Clown, Vito an' even Mitzi, they all know about the Mermaid S.A.C. without me tellin' them anything, so I start at the time that Tommy first begins hangin' around the Club.

ROUND 4

Ever since he's a little kid, Tommie has this thing for Rosie Big Nose Sallie, who naturally was the daughter of Salvatore or Sallie Big Nose Sallie. If Rosie's name woulda been Gwendolyn that woulda been her full, complete name because there would be no other Gwendolyns to mix her up with. But, as in our neighborhood there were more Rosies than lamp-posts, there hadda be a way to tell this Rosie from the others, so what is more natural than a daughter takin' her father's last name?

From the day Tommy first lays eyes on Rosie, which is when they are about six years old, he knows this is the girl for him. And as they get older, which is a very common thing with six-year-olds, this feeling only grows. In order to show his love for Rosie, Tommy does what any red-blooded kid his age would do—he never says a word to her and does not ever look her straight in the eye. Anytime Rosie would walk down the street, Tommy, no matter what he was doin', just freezes like a statue and stays like that until she is gone. But he appoints himself her protector, her guardian angel, her knight in shining armor, her loyal devoted slave—only she don't know none of this. I'm sure she would have felt very good knowing how safe and sound she was. She don't even realize it when circumstances cause Tommy to come to the rescue of his lady fair. They are both in Mrs. Crockett's 8th grade English class, in which neither one of them are exactly over-achievers. Rosie sits in the second row, near the back and Tommy sits in the very last seat two rows over. There is this fat, little kid, Frankie "Footer" Furtado, who was learning life's sweet little mysteries in a very unique way. He dropped his pencil about two hundred times a day, which is very unusual even if you are paralyzed. He would then proceed to bend over, getting his head all the way down to the floor, and go through this very deliberate process of retrievin' his pencil, while his eyes are workin' overtime, like two searchlights scannin' a prison yard, takin' in all the wondrous sights he could see under the skirts of any girl whose kneecaps happened not to be on guard. Unsuspecting Mrs. Crockett would occasionally coo, "We must work on physical as well as mental coordination, Franklin." The fat, little voyeur had the highest marks in the class, besides which he was Mrs. Crockett's eraser monitor, a position in life that all schoolboys strove to attain. Most of the boys in the class, including Tommy, although unable to make the grades that Frankie did, were not so dumb that they didn't realize what he was doing. For the most part, they didn't care, and some even admired such creativity. That is until Mrs. Crockett moves Frankie to the first seat in the third row, so that her shining star can sit right in front of her desk. This gives Frankie a whole new outlook on life and his pencil is now droppin' with a beat like Gene Krupa on the drums. It does not take Tommy too long to realize, in horror, that those two probing beams of Frankie's, are now invading the sanctity of his true love, zeroing in on that which is reserved only for himself, in a very far-off future. Not bein' a kid with a reputation for violence or bein' a bully, Tommy shocks everyone out of their prepositions and past tenses, by boundin' down the aisle separatin' his row from Frankie's and very unceremoniously proceeds to wipe the blackboard clean—which coulda been good or coulda been bad, except it turns out to definitely be bad because he uses Frankie as his eraser. Mrs. Crockett, who is accustomed to more conventional methods of cleaning a blackboard, shrieks, then faints. This is not very helpful, but it does not matter because when she awakens she cannot tell the difference between Frankie and the eraser anyhow—they are both about the same color and shape now.

Tommy, it seems, has drummed himself out of P.S. 188 because he will not give any reason for his actions nor will he apologize and rather than spend a lifetime of detention he chooses to play permanent hookey. This,

however, causes him much pain of the heart as it means
he cannot be certain of seeing Rosie Big Nose Sallie
every day of his life any longer. Rosie, on the other hand,
suffers neither pain nor grief as she has no idea of the
heroic deed perpetrated by her silent admirer. If he
cannot see Rosie because she is in school and he is not,
Tommy figures maybe the next best thing is to be near
her father, Big Nose Sallie, so he now becomes a part
of the sidewalk in front of the Mermaid S.A.C. It does
not matter that persons of the female gender are very
much excluded from the Club's premises; what does
matter is that there is a very strong similarity between
the blood flowing through the veins of Rosie Big Nose
Sallie and Salvatore Big Nose Sallie which leads to a
high degree of possibility that someday Rosie comes
to her father for help or a few bucks or whatever, so
Tommy might as well hang around.

Not too long ago, 'Dwarf' Langella has become the
Number One man at the Club and he is used to seeing
all different kinds of things out front like a coupla folding
chairs, sometimes one or two empty milk cartons, once
in a while even an upside-down pickle barrel which
makes a very good checkerboard table in the
summertime. Although the Dwarf would like the Club
to be somewhat of a class establishment, he can
understand a little garbage here 'n there, and therefore
does not let this stuff bother him. But it starts drivin'
him nuts seein' this same curly-haired, sad-eyed kid

sittin' with his back propped up against the front of the
Club next to the door, never sayin' a word or doin'
anything except lookin' at the tips of his own shoes.

One day the Dwarf comes in and grunts, "Who put
the statue out front?" Everyone looks around and finally
Foghorn Manganaro asks, "What statue, Boss? There
ain't no statue."

"That over there is a statue," explains the Dwarf,
pointing at Tommy through the store window.

"It is not a statue, Boss," contradicts Foghorn, "it is
a boy."

"When something is shaped like a person but it does
not move or walk or talk, then it is a statue", the Dwarf
snarls. "Does he belong to anyone? Does anyone know
him or what he's doin' hangin' out here?"

I feel I should speak up a little. As the youngest
guy in the place, word comes back to me from a coupla
permanent fixtures in P.S. 188 about how Tommy made
Frankie "Footer" into a real frankfurter, an' why he did
it, which although Tommy says nothing, some of the
smarter wise guys figure out anyhow. I tell this story
to the guys but mostly to Big Nose Sallie who looks
and listens but does not say a word or give any indication
of what he is thinking. It is our friend the Clown, here,
who shrugs and says, "What is happening to the youth
of America today? Is this where my hard-earned tax
dollar is going—to educate a generation of perverts?"
The Dwarf squints down at him and says, "In what

dream of yours did you ever pay any tax?"

" 'at's beside the point. It's the principle that counts. Just because the nature of my occupation does not necessitate nor encourage the payment of taxes, doesn't make it right that the taxes I am not paying would be used to clothe and feed a world filled with youthful degenerates."

Goldie, her eyes brimmin' over with real tears, stops me and cries, "didja really say that, Clown, didja? That was so eloquently beautiful!"

"Sure I said it—ya think Sonny would lie about such a touchin' thing?"

Truthfully, I am not a hundred per cent certain that's exactly how the Clown said it, but I am sure that by tellin' it that way it really made the Clown's night. None of the guys in the club back then was impressed like Goldie is—'Foghorn' advises the Clown, "Go tell it to McGillicuddy!", while Fats Suozzo, who believes in creative expression suggests to the Clown, "Shove it in yer ear!" Then Sallie turns an' walks to the door, leavin' the Clown mutterin', "It is no skin off of my nose—it ain't my daughter that got her skirt looked under."

"Hey, Kid," Big Nose Sallie snaps at Tommy, holding the door open, "I wanna talk to ya." Tommy looks up an' if he was a dog you woulda said he changed from a basset hound to a cocker spaniel—he lights up like Babe Ruth just said, "C'mon, Kid, have a catch wit' me."

"You know who I am, Kid?" Sallie asks, leading Tommy into the Club.

"Sure I do. You are Mr. Pignasale."

"You c'n call me Sal or Sallie, that's what everyone does. I understand you got canned from school for defendin' my daughter Rosie's honor, is that right?"

"Sorta," Tommy explains, his face reddening, "but actually I packed it in myself."

"I think maybe you stomped this weasel because you wuz jealous," Sallie teased, "like you wanted to grab a peek yourself and there was not room for all four eyeballs."

"That is very unfair," Tommy stammered, shocked, not believing how Sallie was handling such a delicate subject, "I could not stand by and allow Rosie to be violated."

"Could not let Rosie be what?" Sallie roared. "I think maybe we gotta have a little talk about the birds an' the bees, Kid. Tell me somethin', you got the hots for my Rosie?"

If you ever forgot to turn off your headlights when you parked your car an' you ran your battery down, then you put the key in the ignition an' try to start up the ol' buggy but there just ain't enough juice to turn the engine over—it justs keeps sputterin' aahr–aahr aahr. . . .That's exactly what Tommy sounded like then. But just when it seems like Tommy is going to disintegrate at the age of fourteen, he looks Big Nose

Sallie square in the eye and says," I am not sorry for what I did. I would do it again. I will always protect and defend Rosie." Sallie, who is a big pussycat that cries at the opera and many movies, is suddenly all choked up, with a runny nose. He rumples Tommy's hair an' says, "Your an okay kid. What's your name?"

"Tommy—Tommy Curcio."

ROUND 5

So that is how Tommy gets his foot in the front door of the Club. Maybe it is because it is his daughter who is involved that causes Sallie to see things in Tommy that not too many other people are able to see – I don't know about his mother and father, but let's not count them because that's like askin' if an alcoholic woulda voted against prohibition. Sallie, who believes very strongly in loyalty and honor and respect sees all of these qualities in Tommy. It is because of the way Tommy talks to him, the way he put himself on the line for what he felt was defendin' Rosie's honor an' little things like that which all tie in to Sallie's own code of honor. Now ya gotta understand, Sallie was really a person of high principles – that doesn't mean that his principles were the same as the next guy's, but Sallie took care of his own. Not just from the neighborhood or cronies from the Club, ya see, Sallie had a big family livin' in this village half-way between Napoli and Sorrento. He always made sure they were kept comfortable with whatever food and money he could get to them and once every two years, he would make the trip to Italy like Santa Claus, only without the reindeer. Sallie had very strong feelings and ties for his Motherland, and it was not just because he had family there – it was just his way not to forget where he came from. In fact, most of the guys had family over there and were very proud of where they came from – but don't get me wrong. . . nobody could ever say a bad word about the United States of America around us. We always had the Italian flag and American flag hanging side by side in the Club and don't ask me which we loved more – it was sacrilegious to compare one to the other. It's like askin' a guy to say who he loves more, his mother or his wife, which, when you think about it is really a lot easier to answer.

Anyhow, Sallie sees Tommy as this kid who will not turn his back on you, and it is for this reason that instead of chasin' him he sorta takes the kid under wing. That does not mean he says, "C'mon, Kid, be one of the guys." Instead he lectures Tommy that a fourteen-year old kid belongs in school and how important an education is if you want to get ahead in this world. Tommy points out, not without respect, that a diploma does not even get you to the front of the bread lines and being a student was just not his thing. He did not dare add to that, that the only temptation school held for him was to be near Rosie.

"Well, what d' ya wanna be when you grow up," Big Nose Sallie puts to him? This makes Tommy very uncomfortable. He shuffles his feet and looks down at the floor, "I dunno."

Sallie thinks for a minute, then goes on, "It looks like you're pretty handy with your dukes; that's what sorta graduated you from school. You wanna learn to be a prizefighter?"

Tommy shrugs and answers, "Okay."

At this moment I am very impressed. It is my understanding that one of the most important decisions in a person's life is career selection – even though I have never had the experience myself. I cannot believe all the time and effort that went into the careful examination and analysis of all the options and alternatives available to choose from! "Ya wanna be a fighter?" "Okay."

I mean, what if Sallie picked somethin' else? Just picture him sayin', "Hey, Kid, how wouldja like to be a Rabbi?"

"Yeah, that would be nice – but I ain't Jewish."

"Oh, we c'n take care of that. We get ya some nice, long curly sideburns, a good beaver-skin hat an' a prayer book that ya read backwards – you'd make a nice Rabbi, Kid."

You talk about destiny or the fickle finger of fate. In this case it is the fickle finger of Big Nose Sallie that directs Tommy into the life of bein' a pug.

"It is all very clear now," Goldie deduces, and I am sure she is up well past her bed-time, "Big Nose Sallie makes Tommy into a prizefighter, then Tommy weaves himself a cocoon which he climbs into and goes to sleep for a very long time. When he wakes up, the cocoon pops open and out comes this Tomato Can and lives happily ever after."

"I don't believe it," I am now trying to be a funny person, "she read my mind."

"If I read your mind, Buster, I would have absolutely nothing to say." So much for my bein' a funny person. I now become a hurt and wounded person. "Well, if you don't want me to go on . . ."

"No, no, you go on, Sonny, baby," Mitzi soothes me. "Goldie would be haunted forever if you do not finish telling her what happened to Tommy. And the rest of us, we have invested too many minutes and hours to let you stop now. Anyhow, I only know about Tommy after he went to work for Vito."

There is a moan from Vito, "Do not remind me, please." Meanwhile, the Clown has very quietly slid his chair away from our table and the back of the chair is now touching the table behind ours, from which the people have departed, but being light eaters a large amount of their dinner has been left over. I do not see the Clown's hands moving but little by little the food is disappearing from the table. If Harry Houdini had married a Venus Fly Trap they coulda had a son like the Clown.

"I am really sorry for interrupting," Goldie apologizes, "but if you do not hurry up and finish your story at a reasonable hour it is possible that my clothes will turn to rags and I may lose my slipper running home."

"Then you will thank Sonny," Mitzi laughs, "when a handsome Prince comes knockin' on your door to return your slipper.

"It's better he don't," whispers Goldie, "the Clown'd kill him."

Though I am totally distracted by the Clown's disappearing food act I force myself to explain how Big Nose Sallie does not just turn Tommy into a prizefighter right away. The kid is only fourteen years old. He explains to Tommy how he must learn his trade from the ground floor up, which means he is to box in the amateurs until he has learned all the tricks and he is old enough to turn pro. Tommy says "learning" makes it sound like school and Sallie shoots back, "Maybe, but it is a better school than the school of hard knocks." Tommy, being very respectful of Sallie, does not answer but wonders to himself what can be harder knocks than havin' a job where ya keep gettin' belted?

Sallie brings Tommy to the Police Boys Club in Coney Island on West 8th Street and introduces him to the boxing coach who he instructs to teach Tommy everything there is to know about the manly art of self-defense. Tommy is much impressed at the way the coach "Yes, Sirs" Sallie and the way all the cops at the stationhouse almost snap to attention and salute him, which is easy to understand because Big Nose Sallie and the Dwarf pay them a better salary than they get from the City of New York. That is the way things were until we get this new mayor, Fiorello LaGuardia, who, instead of bein' a real good guy like he shoulda been, writes a whole new set of rules – but that is still a year or so down the road. Right now, Tommy, who is a good listener and follows orders, starts learning his new trade and is spendin' most of his time at the Police Boys Club Gym.

Before you wanna start namin' a Church after Sallie, realize one thing – Big Nose Sallie's favorite charity is Big Nose Sallie. That don't mean that he didn't do right by Tommy or that he wasn't thinkin' about Tommy's interests – I am just sayin' that when Sallie does somethin', it gotta be good for Sallie too. Tommy is no longer hangin' out in front of the Mermaid S.A.C. all day long, which is good because the Dwarf is not the same kind of warm, loving person that Sallie is, and it also possibly gives them, a few years from now, another kid whose buttons they can push when he climbs into the ring. This, too, is good for a guy like Sallie, who likes sittin' at ringside, but is a very nervous individual who does not like to be kept in suspense waitin' to learn how a fight is going to end. Sallie is the kind of guy who, if he read books, which he doesn't, because books are made of paper and Sallie likes things more substantial than paper, unless it is green with the picture of a president, he would have to turn right away to the back to find out what happens. Havin' your own kid in the ring to move around is just like turnin' to the back of the book and know how things are going to end. That is why, most of the time, Sallie and the Dwarf are able to sit at the fights so comfortable and relaxed—no strain, no pain.

It is not too long before Tommy is showin' off what he learned at the local amateur clubs where he gets watches, trophies and little trinkets that he c'n hock fer a few bucks. He has much more fun at the shows they put on at smoker's where a lot of the guys show the kids their appreciation for a good punchout by showering the ring with money. Although Tommy is not exactly a world-beater, he is not a slouch either. He is suddenly a very popular person among his crowd, just by the fact that he is someone in the spotlight, which is reason enough for many kids, and grownups too, to be hangers-on. This does not make Tommy exactly upset or unhappy, because he now sees more of Rosie, who even is in the crowd at many of his fights. Once in a while they go to a movie together. This, obviously, has much more meaning to Tommy than it does to Rosie, who has more dates than a tree in an Arabian oasis.

ROUND 6

After a couple of years, Sallie gets Tommy's report card from his coach and it is pretty good. The only problem is, this is one school where pretty good ain't good enough. The coach explains how Tommy follows all his instructions and does everything asked of him but his punch is just hard enough to pop a soap bubble and his hands are about as fast as the minute hand on a clock. "Not too bad—it coulda been the hour hand," remarks Sallie the optimist. The coach goes on to explain that Tommy will more than hold his own fighting three two-minute rounds in the amateurs, even when he graduates to three minute rounds. But as a pro it may be a different story. Big Nose Sallie did not seem overly perturbed at this as he knew that he and the Dwarf could provide Tommy with plenty of extra power, even if not in his gloves, or else handcuff the kid, whichever seems the more suitable for the particular occasion. It is quite clear to Sallie that Tommy will not be another Tony Canzoneri, but the kid is okay and will serve his purpose.

47

Just about this time I am surprised to discover that although I have had only one year of high school, my education is still continuing. F'r instance, I am learning that it is a very easy and quick trip going from a hero to a bum. It is only natural that you think I am referring to my friend Tommy Curcio. Well,to a degree you are right, but that comes later. Right now I am referring to Il Duce – Benito Mussolini.

Big Nose Sallie has been getting much mail from his family telling what a wonderful leader Mussolini is and how he is rebuilding Italy and making it into a modern industrial power. And the last time Sallie visited there, which was about two years ago he comes back ravin' about the new highways and railways. We are all very proud to hear such things. Sallie and the Dwarf help organize the Coney Island Italian-American Relief Fund whose purpose is to raise money for various Italian projects. Once a month the Mermaid S.A.C. runs a dinner-dance where raffles are sold and there are games of chance to raise more money for the Fund. Everyone's intentions are so honorable that not a penny is skimmed off the top. But now we are getting different stories on the radio and in the newspapers. We begin to hear about prison camps and purges, how some of the people are virtual slaves, that Mussolini is totally whacked out. This is all very distressing to Big Nose Sallie who, together with the Dwarf, decide that rather than send the money over to various government agencies in Italy as was their original intention, Sallie would travel to Italy, smuggling in the money they raised. If he sees the news stories are true and his relatives were afraid to put such things in writing, then they would set up a plan to get the money to all of their relatives, as best they can.

"Oh, I remember those dances, Sonny," the Clown butts in. "That's when they took down the big picture from the foyer wall in the Club."

"I'll bet you remember, Joey," I answered. "If I were you I'd try to forget, though."

The Clown was talking about this dance which was the night after Tommy advanced to the semi-finals in the Golden Gloves and it was also the first time in about two years that Tommy had been to the Club at night. He was feelin' great, almost like it was a celebration party for him, especially since Rosie was going to be there also. As he is walkin' in, two of the guys are just startin' to take down this large picture of Mussolini in uniform that Big Nose Sallie put up about a year ago, but has now ordered removed because the hero has definitely become a bum. Tommy turns to Foghorn Manganaro, who happens to be the nearest person to him, and asks, "Why are they takin' the picture down?"

And the Foghorn answers, "Because he is a bum and does not deserve to be the leader of a great country like Italy, let alone hang on our wall."

Tommy looks shocked. "Tony Galento is the leader of Italy?"

Big Nose Sallie is standing nearby and hears this.
"You oughta be ashamed of yourself. That is Benito
Mussolini – Il Duce – a much bigger bum than Tony
Galento. You oughta try lookin' at the front of a
newspaper once in a while, not just the sport section."
The picture is gone and Tommy is very red-faced, when
at that moment the Clown walks through the front door,
takes one look at the now empty wall and blurts out,
"Hey, what happened to the picture of Tony Galento?"
I guess that is what is called redemption. "Aw, don't
make fun of me," the Clown mutters. "I still say Mussolini
and Tony Galento were the same person!"

What the Clown does makes Tommy feel a little
better and he thinks it'll be a pretty good night after
all. But it is not; in fact it goes from bad to Disasterville
for him. He hardly gets the chance to dance or talk with
Rosie at all. Every time he gets near her some bozo
is either cuttin' in or buttin' in, which it turns out was
probably better than when he finally does get to dance
with her. It is true that stepping on someone's feet a
number of times does not necessarily put that person
in the very best of moods and that may be why when
Tommy says, "What'ja think of my fight last night – I
felt real lucky to win", Rosie cracks her chewin' gum,
"I felt you were very lucky to win, too." Tommy,
recognizing that Rosie was his girl, even though Rosie
did not share in this knowledge, knows her response
was open to interpretation but he also does decide to

be more careful about steppin' on her feet. "It is very exciting being in the semifinals, knowing you will be cheering me on from ringside next week."

"Unless they are holding the Golden Gloves in the middle of the Atlantic Ocean, the only cheering I will be doing is if they are having a shuffleboard tournament on the deck of the steamship that is taking me and my father to Italy." Although he had been in nearly fifty amateur fights, Tommy, until now had no idea what it felt like to be knocked senseless. He knew he should be telling her about this terrific dream he was having almost every night and how such a wonderful dream should not be ruined. He should be telling her that this dream was so great that it was impossible that he dreamt this whole dream in his own head all by himself. Dreams get fuzzy sometimes but he was sure it started out with "A Cecil B. DeMille Dream" an' the whole dream is in technicolor, and then there he is, Tommy, in the center of this ring with the announcer holding his hand high in victory as the new Golden Gloves champion and there is Rosie, fighting her way into the ring, trying to embrace him while he is shouting into the microphone, "I did it for you, Rosie and for the United States of America!" He knew this is what he should tell her and when she heard such a sensational dream she would definitely have tears running down her cheeks and change her mind about sailing to Italy. He looked Rosie straight in the eyes and his head felt like it was filled with cotton as he got up the courage to make his mouth work, "I hope that the waves are not too rough in the ocean and you have a very nice trip."

So Rosie goes off to Italy with Big Nose Sallie and Tommy goes to the semi-final round of the Golden Gloves. All the guys from the Mermaid S.A.C. are there to root for Tommy except for the Dwarf, who says he does not go to watch amateur fights because they are too unprofessional. I still remember that fight pretty good. We all cheered every time Tommy threw a punch but he missed them both. We showed up because we knew Tommy was supposed to fight that night, but I don't know why Tommy showed up because I don't think he knew he was supposed to fight that night. To me it seems that Tommy is hunting butterflies, which I cannot understand, because the St. Nicholas arena, where the Golden Gloves semi-finals are being held, although a very old building is a completely indoor establishment – I mean with walls and a ceiling – a place where butterflies should not be but yet Tommy is lookin' to this side, to that side, up at the ceiling, down at the floor, everywhere but at the other guy in the ring with him. Meanwhile, this guy, believe me, is not chasin' butterflies. He is very busy bein' a social director – introducing both of his hands to Tommy's head, between whom a very close, personal attachment develops.

Not wishing to keep anyone in suspense, I am now informing everyone that, surprisingly, Tommy did not win the fight and as good buddies we saw our duty to console him as we knew he had to be very depressed at this moment. We told him that getting to the semifinals in the Gloves was nothin' to be ashamed of and we wanted to celebrate with him by takin' him wherever he wanted to go. What we had in mind was maybe a real hot burlesque show, a good spaghetti house on Mulberry Street, or maybe even a swell joint like the Havana-Madrid. "Wherever ya wanna go, Tommy Baby," Fats Suozzo says, givin' him a friendly shot in the arm to show he loves him. "It's your night."

For the first time that night Tommy stops lookin' for butterflies. "Okay. Let's go to Italy." This he says without battin' an eyelash or crackin' a smile. Without lookin' up the price, immediately we realize this would cost us more even than the Havana-Madrid. But what Tommy says makes all the brains in the room go to work at the same time. There is a lot of silent whirring and clicking and registering inside of all of our heads and in a matter of seconds each brain spits out the answer to the person it is attached to—Tommy is in love with Rosie Big Nose Sallie!

Personally, I do not think it is such a good idea for Tommy to have such high ambitions. This is not only because Rosie's head is not screwed on very tightly but also due to the fact that Big Nose Sallie has made it known many times that his daughter must marry a person worthy of the Pignasale status, which means like a person from Bath Beach, Bay Ridge, Bensonhurst or maybe even Rego Park but definitely not Coney Island. Being sensitive human beings we do not let it be known to Tommy that we have discovered it is a wounded heart that is causing him to be such a depressed person. And because of such depression Tommy chooses to go nowhere if he cannot go to Italy. So our big treat now becomes all of us pilin' into a Yellow Cab and takin' Tommy home in style instead of goin' with the BMT.

It is then that Foghorn Manganaro gets this brainstorm of an idea which I must admit, I did not think too much of at the time. However, we must do something before Tommy jumps off Steeplechase Pier. Foghorn manages to let us know his plan without Tommy noticing or hearing anything, which is not overly difficult as Tommy's head is off visiting places that only Flash Gordon and Buck Rogers have been to before.

Around the corner from Nathan's Hot Dogs, between Surf Avenue and the Bowery, there is this Gypsy fortune teller, Madame Chardova, who has previously brightened our fortunes on numerous occasions. That is because this most versatile seer not only looks into the future, she is also willing to help make the future. She, who has the ability to read your palm, is willing to do much more than that if you are willing to grease her palm. There is more than one voluptuous young maiden who relented to the previously undetected and unnoticed charm of her evening's date after Madame

Chardova foretold of the wondrous future awaiting her together with her Prince Charming if she only knew how to satisfy and comfort him in this hour of loneliness and need. Tommy, due to his tenderness of years, had not yet heard of this fabled Gypsy.

While the rest of us felt the urgency of devouring a hot dog, Foghorn went ahead to Madame Chardova's to set the stage which we hoped would help bring Tommy back to the world. Tommy was a most unwilling subject at first, but when we told him he might even find out who was going to be the mother of his children, a team of wild horses couldn't have held him back. When we got to Madame Chardova's, we gave her a buck, which was just for show, because we knew Foghorn had already taken care of her. Tommy sits down at the round table opposite her while the rest of us sit on chairs in her small foyer which is her waiting room and from where we are able to hear pretty good. Madame Chardova is a very large, heavy woman who never leaves her seat. Her long, black curly hair is not combed, just tied back with a ribbon and she has no makeup on her lined olive skin. She has a hooked nose like Dick Tracy and her eyes, although opened very wide, are a soft gray and make her look as though she is asleep with her eyes open. She asks Tommy for his St. Christopher's medal which is around his neck, clasps it tightly in her right hand, closes her eyes and for about two minutes does not make a sound; she seems not even to be breathing.

For a moment I am worried that maybe she is dead and would it be unethical to roll a corpse. After all, we did invest good money in this session.

Just then I hear her speaking in a very low, confidential whisper to Tommy. "I see you now, standing in a garden – the sun is shining and you are alone – now flowers begin to appear. You must like gardens, right?"

"I don't think so. I got hay fever."

Madame Chardova continued. "Now the flowers are moving about you – one by one they approach you and you send them on their way. There is a tulip – it leaves. Now a daffodil – it leaves." She repeats this with all different flowers, until, "This next one is a rose. Slowly, it comes to you – something is different – this one, the rose, you do not send away – nor will it be sent away." Now Tommy is leaning forward, drinking in every word. It looks like he wants to shake Madame Chardova to make her talk faster. The gypsy drones on, "This rose is blossoming in your presence. It is more than a flower. . ."

Tommy blurts out, "Sure it is, it's not a flower, doncha get it? It's Rosie. . .it's my girl Rosie!"

"SSssh," the gypsy holds up a restraining hand to quiet him. "You must not break the spell." There is another moment of complete silence, except for Tommy's rapid wheezing gasps of breath. "Now something is happening," the fortune teller goes on, "the rose is disappearing – no, it is not disappearing – it is changing into a girl – a woman...."

"What does she look like?", pleads Tommy, needing further assurance.

"It is very difficult," Madame Chardova covers up, "she is wearing a white gown...a wedding gown and her face is covered with a bridal veil. The garden has now become a chapel and a young man is standing at the altar...the young man is you. The bride is being escorted down the aisle by...it seems to be just a face...a disembodied face. I do not understand. Now part of the face is fading...yes, the ears are gone, now the chin is gone and so is the mouth. I cannot make anything of this. You must help me. Only part of a face is now escorting the bride to you. The eyes vanish leaving only ...."

"A nose. A nose," Tommy shouts, glorying in this wondrous moment, "it is a nose!"

"Yes," Madame Chardova concurs, "it is a nose. A very big nose. What does it mean?"

"It is my father-in-law – Big Nose Sallie," Tommy shrieks in joy. "It is my father-in-law!" What a job Foghorn did filling in Madame Chardova!

"Oh, of course," says the gypsy closing her eyes and slumping in her chair, pretending she was once again in a trance, thinking that there must be a better way to earn a living.

There was no keeping Tommy down now. He was so high it was like we took him to Kiddie Land and had the balloon man pump him up with helium. Now he knew that Rosie was his. It was like a match made in heaven. I was just hopin' that the Foghorn, who looked brilliant right now, did the right thing. Certainly no one was able to fault him because Tommy's life jumped right back to normal which meant spendin' most of his time at the Gym, havin' a couple of fights a month, and most of the time just daydreamin' about Rosie, who, with Big Nose Sallie, had returned after spendin' two months in Italy. Tommy decided not to say anything to Rosie about Madame Chardova. He musta figured their impending marriage would be much more exciting to her if it were a complete surprise, which it looked like it would definitely have to be.

ROUND 7

Even with Tommy winnin' most of his fights it is still the amateurs and it is beginnin' to look like no way is he goin' to set the world on fire, not with a mountain of oil-soaked rags and an acetelyn torch. But he still has a pretty good shot at doin' more'n okay because as long as the Dwarf an' Big Nose Sallie steer him he has what the sportswriters like to call "that intangible something extra".

If Tommy is doin' a bit of all right, the same does not hold true for everyone else. First, when Big Nose Sallie gets back from Italy he makes it sound like if the Three Stooges wanted to make it a quartet, Mussolini gets first crack at the job. And Italy's war against Ethiopia was like the New York Yankees takin' on the P.S. 188 punch-ball team. Only bullets and bombs are not baseballs and bats and to the rest of the world it was a disgrace. The Italian flag came down in the Mermaid S.A.C. and now the American flag hung alone. The Dwarf and Sallie make it known that all the money raised by the Coney Island Italian-American Relief

Fund from now on will be used to help our relatives over there; none of it will go to any agency of the Italian government.

Meanwhile, raisin' any kind of money was becomin' a little more difficult for the Dwarf and Sallie, and Vito, also. The Dwarf had been doin' very nicely placin' pinball machines and small countertop gambling machines in all the local candy stores and bars. Me an' a few of the other guys would go around placin' the machines, makin' the collections a couple times a week and changin' the machines every two or three months so people would not get bored with the same action.

Vito, who always had a nose fer business, opened up a game arcade that only had games of chance. He called it a coffee shop because he had a coffee counter with some stale doughnuts and Yankee Doodles to make the place legit. Everything is fine until we get this two-foot-three-inch mayor, Fiorello LaGuardia who the Dwarf says is wonderful because he always wanted to have a mayor he could really keep in his hip pocket. At the beginning, we feel he is not a bad guy; he is a friend of the working man and comes from the streets just like us so he must know the score. Well, we soon find out that if he knows the score, it is not in our favor. He has this thing against free enterprise and the American way of life. He starts rantin' an' ravin' that pinball machines 'n such are stealin' old ladies' milk money an' school children's lunch money. But it is not that he just says they gotta go. He wants to show the whole world that he's gonna make them go.

Vito had this warehouse on Cropsey Avenue that he used to store and repair pinball machines. In fact Vito supplied the Dwarf with his machines and serviced them for him. Anyhow, on this particular night Vito gets a call to hurry down to the warehouse because there is a major problem. When Vito gets there he cannot believe what he sees. The place is crawlin' with cops and they are bein' led by Mayor LaGuardia himself, with a hatchet in his hand, as do most of the cops. Vito, you tell 'em what happened.

Vito shrugs and picks up the story, "My first thought is, my mind gotta be playin' tricks on me. This guy wantsa become President and he is doin' the George Washington bit, only there is no cherry tree here. In another minute he is not George Washington anymore, now he is like Teddy Roosevelt leadin' the troops on a charge up Bunker Hill..."

"I do not think Teddy Roosevelt was at Bunker Hill," I correct him.

"It does not matter," snaps Vito, "it is the thought not the deed. Anyhow, they are all swingin' their hatchets, choppin' up my pinball machines while all the newspaper fotogs and movie cameramen are havin' a field day. I am screamin' an' shoutin' but it does no good. Then the reporters start askin' me questions, an' me, like a dummy—I am so mad, I answer them an' it is splashed all over the papers the next day. One reporter asks, "Mayor LaGuardia said–'Let this be an example to all purveyors of gambling devices in this city.' What do you think of the Little Flower's actions?"

"Little Flower," I laugh. "What Little Flower?" This was the newsmen's loving name for LaGuardia. "He is a stinkweed, not a little flower!" 'Even after all this time I do not enjoy talkin' about it. You go on, Sonny.'

What Vito has described is just the beginning of fireworks the likes of which you would not believe if Chinese New Year and the Fourth of July wuz celebrated at the same time. He is not called the Fuse because he is the kind of person who would come to your assistance if your lights blew out. I say that with the utmost of affection and respect...because I know I better–Only kiddin', Vito.

Vito is not lookin' to have an ulcer, so he makes sure never to let anything be bottled up inside him. You do not look at Vito and say, I wonder what he really thinks on the inside–what Vito thinks on the inside he shows pretty good on the outside. He don't leave nothin' to your imagination. Anyhow, maybe it is Ulcer Prevention Week–but whatever it is, it is not Self-Control Week– Vito goes absolutely bananas. At least when Vito goes bananas he does it in the right place. A couple days after our Mayor's big smash in Coney Island there is some commotion in the Monkey House at the Prospect Park Zoo that gets good picture coverage in the middle

pages of the Daily News and Daily Mirror. It seems
that the brass plate, the one that tells who is residing
in that particular cage, on the front of the baboon cage
has been switched. What is there now, reads "Fiorellus
LaGuardius". The sole occupant of that cage, a cute fella
when ya get right down to it, just walks aroun' scratchin'
his head. Ya gotta assume he is not in on this and it
is becomin' obvious he ain't gonna talk. And if he could
talk I am sure he would tell ya it is strictly a coincidence,
a very strong one to be sure, that the chief zookeeper
of the Monkey House is named Vinnie Fusillo, who just
happens to be Vito's second cousin.

The fact that Mayor LaGuardia makes no response
to this act of provocation does not in the least deter
our good friend, the indomitable Vito. He is now on the
move like the cavalry in a Hoot Gibson western. The
day after the Monkey House caper, the Times Square
traffic, which does not exactly flow like a river under
the best of conditions, gets clogged up like your kitchen
sink when ya throw chicken bones down the drain. Ya
see, our Mayor has little characteristics that separate
him from the average man on the street. It may not
make him better or worse but it does make him
different. First, he loves a good fire. He goes to all of
them—without no marshmallows, mickeys or wieners—
just with his Fire Chief's hat, a fireman's raincoat and,
you got it, his hatchet, again. The newspapers are always
puttin' his picture in at this fire, at that fire. . .great

copy! It is true, there are many people living away from home in establishments with very soft walls because they, too, loved chasing fire engines, but they did not have their own hatchets. So the traffic does not move and that is because on Broadway, on Seventh Avenue and on Forty-Second Street, there are a bunch of very small people, like midgets and dwarfs dressed in firemen's hats, raincoats and wavin' itty-bitty hatchets; on the back of their raincoats is stencilled in yellow, "Mayor LaGuardia", and they are runnin' aroun', knockin' on car windows, screechin', "Where's the fire? Where's the fire?" "Tell me where the fire is – I am your Mayor." Some drivers were angry but most were splittin' their sides laughin'; they were laughin' so hard, they could not drive.

Midgets must be very tough people because a few of 'em got arrested for disruptin' traffic, but not one of 'em would tell who put them up to it. Vito did not step forward and take any bows, but none o' the guys in our neighborhood got headaches tryin' to figure it out. Again, the Mayor says nothin'. But the next morning when the Mayor arrives at City Hall and is greeted by a stack of busted-up pinball machines dumped on the front sidewalk with a note attached, "A GIFT TO THE MAYOR FROM AN UNKNOWN ADMIRER", the storm troopers are sent to Coney Island and Vito is picked up. Although Vito is treated very leniently by the court – he is fined a couple hundred dollars, which he says is less than it would have cost to cart the machines away—the Dwarf feels it is time to step into the picture.

The Dwarf is not one to mince words—you don't have to mince words when you can mince people. Maybe it is because Vito is a celebrity now, sorta like a Robin Hood, or maybe it's just that the Dwarf really got a kick outta what Vito carried on, just like the rest of us did, but he does not give orders to Vito, he talks to him man-to-man. He pats Vito on the cheek. "Vito, all of these things you are doing to our poor Mayor makes us begin to believe you are not a very forgiving person."

Vito smiles at the Dwarf, "That is not so, Donato. I'm for giving the little bum everything that's comin' to him." The Dwarf goes on to explain to Vito how it is not to anyone's advantage to carry out a vendetta against LaGuardia and how it is easier to catch bees with honey. "Vito, you got a new restaurant," the Dwarf is talking about the Villa Vito which Vito and his brother Gino opened six months ago in Bay Ridge, "and you are a successful businessman at a time when it is very hard to make a buck. You know the City can make things very difficult for you. You're too smart, Vito. You're too smart."

That was one point Vito would not argue. But, also he realized it was true. The Villa Vito was a tremendous success in the short time it was doing business; the coffee shop/game room was just a toy. The reason the Villa Vito was doing so good is that Vito has a very sharp nose for business. He was always different than most of the guys at the Club. Hangin' around, playin' games and drinkin' espresso was not for him. Vito was not a relaxer, he always hadda be on the move doin' somethin'. The Villa Vito was a stroke of genius, but also a real gamble. Vito and Gino had renovated and rebuilt a large mansion that they bought from an estate and converted it into a palatial restaurant with magnificent grounds and landscaping. Doing something like this in the middle of a depression was insanity— but not in Vito's mind. He geared this restaurant to those people who had somehow escaped or benefitted from the Depression. His menu was so elaborate and expensive, that to most people it was a fairy tale. It was not called 'dinner' at the Villa Vito, it was called a dining experience, a culinary adventure. Celebrities flocked there just to be able to say they dined at the Villa Vito. Each dining room represented a region or city in Italy—there was the Venetian Room, the Tuscany Room, Capri Room and the bar and lounge area was called Via Veneto. Gino handled the daytime operations while Vito was the one to oversee everything at night. So, usually Vito was a free soul during the day and loved to spend most of his time at the track. Most people were very surprised to find out that Vito was "the Vito" of the Villa Vito because he was always a real down-to-earth guy. The landscaping of the Villa Vito made it look like a replica of Signorina's Square in Florence, complete with copies of the statues. When you drove up to the restaurant you entered from Shore Road onto a curved drive that led you to the canopied entrance from where parking valets would attend to your car and a doorman would greet you. Everything about the Villa Vito was impressive.

After his meeting with the Dwarf, Vito spends a lot of time thinkin' about what the Dwarf said and he decides Langella was not just a little right—he was very, very right and Vito knows he has to make amends. Ya gotta understand—Vito is not a half-way guy—when he does somethin' it is usually an all the way thing. So now it is his decision to throw this big bash at the Villa Vito honoring Fiorello H. LaGuardia, who in Vito's eyes is no longer such a bad guy after all. The only problem that Vito can see is that if the Mayor is told that the dinner is to be in his honor and that Vito Fusillo is in any way involved there will certainly be an empty seat at the dais. So Vito decides on a fund-raising Dinner-Dance for the Coney Island Italian-American Relief Fund with Mayor LaGuardia to be invited as the guest speaker and Vito's name will nowhere be mentioned. Nor is it anyone's business to know that whatever money is raised by the Coney Island Italian-American Relief Fund is ear-marked for the sole use of the families in Italy of the guys in the Club.

Vito gives first preference to neighborhood kids to work the valet parking service, so as soon as Tommy is eighteen he is lookin' to make some extra change by workin' nights for Vito who already promised him the job but never told him he was supposed to know how to drive. Tommy already had two pro fights an' won both by decisions. It may not have hurt him that Sallie hand-picked the two opponents, whose managers were both very friendly to Big Nose Sallie. But it is an exciting time for Tommy—they even throw him a little shindig at the Club after his first fight an' the kid is glowing. Not so much that he wins the fight, but mainly because Rosie Big Nose Sallie is hangin' on him like a drunk to a lamppost. I guess bein' in the spotlight does have its rewards.

ROUND 8

It is not my intention here to imply that life cannot be a bowl of cherries but on the other hand I must confess that I am a strong believer in what goes up must come down. I am not a negative person despite the rumor, probably spread by some former unrequited paramour, that at my wedding, when the good priest asked, "Do you take this woman for better or for worse...," I mumbled, "Why? You got a refund policy, Father?" It is totally untrue. I accepted my fate without utterin' a word. But I am a realist. And I am sure, after what happens, Tommy is a realist, too.

It all comes together on this big night where Mayor LaGuardia is the secret guest of honor at this grand affair at the Villa Vito. The Fuse really outdoes himself for this one. The grounds are freshly manicured, the building is scrubbed so clean that a dust mote would have to think twice before settling down there. The uniforms of all the employees are laundered and starched and there is a string quartet playing classical music on the lawn facing the entrance....Excuse me, everyone. I see Goldie is havin' trouble holdin' her water right now...She's buggin' the Clown, "How's he know that? How's he know that?" Well, for one night in my life I am gainfully employed—off the books, of course—as the Assistant Doorman. Every time the Number One Doorman has to go pee or indulge in some similar pursuit, I am the pinch-hittin' Doorman, with my own uniform and all. In fact I have my picture taken which I bring over to my mother's house—my old lady, she got a picture of me from the wedding, she don't need no more—an' my mother is so proud she cries all night; she don't have the picture after that night because she mails it to my Uncle Ignacio in Spoleto and tells him I am a General in the United States Army. My Uncle Ignacio writes back that she must be very proud of me and it is such a beautiful uniform that in Spoleto even the Doormen do not have such beautiful uniforms.

Anyhow, like I said, Vito pulled out all the stops, but his piece de resistance was a larger-than-life statue that he had commissioned of Mayor LaGuardia, which was to be unveiled on this night. It is under wraps right next to where the string quartet is playing, on the lawn facing the entrance. It seems that every celebrity and important person in New York is turning out for this event. In fact, people were comin' from outta town. The Dwarf gets a call from Squinty DiPalma, the Big Boss of Philadelphia, who asks if the Dwarf will do him this favor and get him a reservation at the Villa Vito for what should be a real excitin' evenin'. They don't do things on such a large scale in Philly. The Dwarf lets Squinty know he owes him one.

As the Dinner Hour approaches, Vito makes the rounds inspectin' all his employees and instructin' each one what he expects of him and how he should perform his duty. I never seen Vito so formal before. Tommy is assigned to stand at the head of the drive and direct each car as it enters the grounds. This is not what Tommy wanted because ya make the real money parkin' the cars an' gettin' tips and it was easy to see that a lot of this crowd was big tippers. Tommy figures he knows a lot of the guys there an' maybe later on he c'n switch with someone, after they teach him to drive, of course. One of the guys workin' there was Frankie Furtado, who Tommy had dismantled over four years ago, defending Rosie Big Nose Sallie's honor. In all that time Tommy has had neither the occasion nor the desire to speak to Frankie. He felt maybe it was time now to bury the hatchet. And Frankie felt likewise only I believe it was his idea to bury it somewhere in Tommy's back. He assured Tommy there were no hard feelings – they were kids then – and he very graciously taught Tommy everything there was to know about drivin' a car in what is called a real crash course.

Kids are really very intelligent people, much more so than grownups in many situations. F'r instance, kids realize the importance of bein' able to call back a moment of your life. A kid's philosophy is that everyone is entitled to make one mistake an' have the opportunity to call it back an' get a second chance. I remember as a kid growin' up on the streets of Coney Island, playin' in whatever game it happened to be at the time, they were all important, and suddenly, there was that mistake, that moment of your life that hadda be called back, an' ya shout out, "Hindoo!" or "Do-Over!" or "Chinese Misforgets!" They all meant the same an' they all served the same purpose—you bought a second chance—you were entitled to it. Tommy shoulda been able to call out "Hindoo" that night but it don't work once you're a grownup.

Frankie Furtado is workin' the booth with the key board. As each car is parked the attendant turns the key over to Frankie who hangs it on the peg for the spot where that car was parked. Also a job with no tips but it is this booth that coordinates the entire valet parking service. The cars are now comin' in hot 'n heavy and Vito's nephew, Benny DeLuca yells over to Frankie for more parking attendants. Frankie, in turn, shouts to Tommy to leave the directin' job an' come work as a parking attendant. As Tommy trots up the drive, more than a little apprehensive at what he is about to tackle, there is a great deal of gasping and oohs and ahs as this canary-yellow Auburn Boattail Speedster makes its way to the entrance with Squinty DiPalma at the wheel. Just as he reaches the curb there is a polite smattering of applause, and Squinty, in appreciation of such a display of respectful recognition, doffs his cap to the admiring crowd. But the applause is not for him; immediately following Squinty's flamboyant sports car is a Packard Town Car which is carrying Mayor Fiorello H. LaGuardia. Benny DeLuca, seeing the Mayor, starts barking orders, "Awright, let's park the Auburn, someone park the Auburn so Hizzoner can pull up!" Meanwhile, Squinty is slightly a hypertense person, "I do not like anyone drivin' my car. I will park it myself."

"No, no, fella," Benny insists, having no idea who he was speakin' to. "We have a very capable, experienced staff of attendants here. The parking area is not accessible to our guests. Please just relax an' enjoy the evenin'. Frankie, give this gentleman the stub for his car an' get it parked so the Mayor's chauffeur can pull up."

"I don't know," Squinty mutters, but he steps back and surrenders his car.

"Go on, Tommy," Frankie smiles. "It is your baby. Take the Auburn up the hill." Tommy slides in behind the wheel and repeats to himself everything that Frankie told him, "Clutch in...slide the shift...letter 'H'... neutral is middle... slide it down and towards you...foot off clutch..." and the Auburn zoomed backwards! There was a hideous grinding and clashing of metal against metal. Both the Auburn and Packard lurched like two stallions locked in combat. Tommy, certain he was already dead, threw the shift straight forward now and the Auburn bolted across the drive; the string quartet, which very appropriately had been playing Schubert's Eighth Symphony, which is the Unfinished Symphony, made an on-the-spot determination that there would be no more music for this night and scattered for their lives; the alabaster Fiorello LaGuardia did not fare nearly as well although it stood its ground bravely against the onslaught of the charging Auburn. When the dust cleared, the Auburn looked more like an accordion than a car and the new statue looked like the Headless Horseman without a horse. The noise, which sounded somethin' like the end of the world is probably gonna sound like, brought Vito runnin' out of his office where he was hiding just in time to hear this clunk-clunk an' see Frankie Furtado lift up this head that was bouncing down the drive, smile and recite, "Alas, poor Fiorello. I knew him well." It took Vito about five seconds to realize it was the statue's head an' not the Mayor's. The second the Mayor, from inside the smokin' Packard with the bashed-in radiator sees Vito he is sure it is an assassination attempt on his life and screams to his chauffeur, "Let's get the Hell out of here, Victor. Run for our lives!"

Victor, who now fully believes this to be the very last day of his life, throws the car into reverse and somehow negotiates the curved drive full tilt in reverse. I gotta be objective—it was a better job of drivin' than Tommy coulda done.

Well, if Victor thinks it is the last day of his life, what could Tommy be thinkin'? He is probably wishin' that yesterday was the last day of his life. At this moment I am being very studious. I am counting every vein in Vito's neck and head. Truthfully, this is not a very difficult assignment as they are all bulging out in a way that makes it easy to see and count them from a very far distance. As Vito's veins de-bulge he starts stammerin' and sputterin', pointin' his finger at Tommy, who is sittin' in the crunched Auburn examinin' the rubble left in his wake, "You, get outta that car. You do not drive cars here anymore."

"I guess I'm fired, huh, Vito?" Tommy asks, climbing out of the car.

"No, you are not fired. You are gonna work off what you cost me, which means you may have to live to be a thousand years old. But you do not drive cars." He then turns to Frankie Furtado an' shouts, "Put that dopey head down an' get outta the booth." Then back to Tommy, "You, you work the booth an' the key board. From now on you are on Car Key Duty. You understand. That is your only job. You are my Car Key Duty Boy. Benny, d'you follow what I'm sayin'? Tommy don't drive no more cars. He is strictly the Car Key Duty Boy. Got it?"

Benny tries very hard to keep a straight face but he manages and answers, "Yeah, sure, Uncle Vito. From now on Tommy is the Car Key Duty Boy." Then Benny turns around to the rest of the attendants and roars, "Okay, fellas, shape up. From now on Tommy Curcio is the Car Key Duty Boy. He don't park cars. Treat him with the proper respect." All the guys are jumpin' on pretty good now. "Okay Cockie Doody Boy" was the call of the day.

Meanwhile, all of this saved Tommy's life because Squinty DiPalma had definitely decided to kill Tommy just a few minutes ago but now Squinty was layin' on the sidewalk laughin' so hard he was cryin'. You could not kill somebody called the Cockie Doody Boy. It would be unfair to the rest of the world. Wait'll they hear this one in Philly!

So what, you are probably thinkin'? Tommy's life is not over. It is not the worst thing in the world that coulda happened. Well, in reference to Vito you are partially correct. Vito is a guy with a conscience who blows really hot and then really cold. After he has time to think things over he does not force Tommy to be his indentured slave. In fact a couple days after this disaster, Vito goes to the track with an inside tip from the Dwarf an' makes back everything he lost that night plus a little vigorish on top. Also, he decides, it was never meant to be between himself an' the Mayor. He does have a memento; he has kept LaGuardia's statuesque head, had it scooped out on top an' it is now an ashtray on Vito's desk an' Vito is always braggin' that we got a Mayor who really uses his head. All this does not mean that he runs out an' buys Tommy a charm bracelet but he winks at the kid an' says, "G'wan, Kid, we're square. I know ya didn't mean it. But remember one thing—ya gotta go someplace, use the trolley car."

The way things go with Vito makes Tommy very much relieved and it is only natural that Tommy feels if it goes good with Vito he can chalk the whole thing up as one very big, very bad night that he manages to live through—but that is all—and now he can continue with his life just like it was before. Only Tommy soon learns, much to his displeasure, that Vito is the up side to what comes out of his Big Bad Night. It is not that all people have cruel streaks like they get a kick out of pulling wings off flies. It's just that they seem to get their biggest kicks bein' able to laugh at somebody who screws up or does somethin' really weird. So Tommy becomes a most reluctant celebrity; he is the star of a show he does not even want to be in. He is now a main attraction wherever he goes just like a "Wrong Way" Corrigan or one of the freaks on the Coney Island Midway. As soon as he walks into a room someone gives out with, "Hey, it's the Cockie Doody Boy" an' there's a bunch of laughs an' snatches of explainin' here 'n there to whoever might not have heard the story of Tommy's famous drive at the Villa Vito.

This does not infer that Tommy is not a likeable person or that his company is not welcome. People just think of him a little differently now. He would much rather they thought of him as Tommy the Prizefighter instead of Tommy the-guy-who-crashed-two-cars-and-smashed-the-Mayor's-statue. He holds out the hope that this is a very temporary stage of his life because he knows all those things like "fame is fleeting" and "tempus fugit" but it is unfortunate that he must learn that in his case "fleeting" and "fugit" seem to get stuck in the mud. After a while Tommy starts makin' himself scarce at places where he used to be pretty much a regular. He does not let on that he is hurt or bothered but he is only a human being and therefore it is very natural to assume that he is not exactly floating on cloud nine. With all the Good Time Charlies pokin' fun at him, Tommy still does not seem angry at anyone, realizin' he would probably be actin' the same way if it was someone else who took the ride in Squinty's car. But it does come out in a couple of conversations that Tommy now believes that Frankie Footer intentionally set the stage for him by giving him wrong instructions on the different positions of the shift stick. Even knowin' this, he makes no move to run Frankie through a meat grinder but instead blames himself for bein' dumb enough to listen to a guy who does not exactly keep Tommy's picture on his mantle place.

Every Fourth of July we have this big cook-out and celebration on the beach an' I put my nose where it shouldn't be by twistin' Tommy's arm to come along an' join the fun. Only as soon as Tommy gets there a bunch

of the guys led by Frankie start singin' what at first
I think is "Yankie Doodle Came to Town" because that's
what it sounds like–but it ain't. Everyone starts
heehawin' like a barn full of donkeys listenin' to their
cousin jackasses singin'

> "Cockie Doodie came to town drivin' Squinty's
> Auburn.
> Smashed into Fiorello's car and gave the
> Mayor heartburn.
> Cockie Doodie keep it up till the Mayor gets
> calmer.
> Then all you got to worry about is a guy
> named Squinty DiPalma!"

Only Tommy is not laughin' out loud. He just stands
there with this silly grin on his face knowin' that Frankie
Furtado, while no George Gershwin, was obviously the
composer of this piece. I am certain that this will drive
Tommy to action because if it does not, what will? It
does not and I soon find out what will.

It is the sight of Frankie sittin' around the campfire
holdin' hands with Rosie Big Nose Sallie while he is
toastin' marshmallows on a stick he is holdin' in his other
hand that finally winds up Tommy's motor. I am
watching his nostrils flaring like someone is pumpin' air
through him with a bellows. It is obvious that he cannot
stand the sight of Frankie's mouth and Rosie's mouth
on the same stick. Once again his future bride is being
violated by this creep. Frankie has become quite

a celebrity since the night at the Villa Vito about which he has been braggin' to everyone how he was the one who set the stage for Tommy's ride, and no one is more impressed than Rosie Big Nose Sallie. Everyone stops whatever they were doin', watchin' Tommy shuffle slowly in the sand, lookin' somethin' like the Frankenstein monster on the loose, headin' straight for Frankie. Frankie gotta be thinkin' deja vu as he lets go of Rosie's hand and pointing his marshmallow stick at Tommy, his eyes buggin' outta his head, croaks, "You better watch out, Tommy. I am warning you – I am a student trained in the Charles Atlas method of Dynamic Tension. Do not think you can kick sand in my face an' get away with it."

Tommy obviously is not frozen by fear but neither does he pulverize Frankie which is everyone's expectation and the wish of most of us. Instead, he snatches the stick which Frankie is holdin' like Douglas Fairbanks set for a major swordplay, and says, "You have been indulgin' in something that is most unhygienic." He then proceeds to slide the two smolderin' marshmallows off the stick and mush them right square in Frankie's puss. Without sayin' another word he turns and walks away, leavin' Frankie sputterin', "You are only fortunate that I am restraining myself because there is a lady present."

I was beginnin' to feel most despondent over Tommy's fall from grace, especially since, I am embarrassed to admit, on a couple of occasions, even I joined in on razzin' the kid. I guess it seems to be the natural thing to do, to pounce on a guy when he is down. But now I know the kid needs a friend or at least some Big Brother kind of advice. It is most disturbin' seein' him carry the torch for such a dizzy dame like Rosie Big Nose Sallie who does not even know Tommy is alive an' believes that any guy around is there strictly for her pleasure. She is a good-lookin' kid with a pretty good shape, this I gotta admit, but there is no furniture in her attic; the upstairs is absolutely empty. An' whatever else Big Nose Sallie gave her, it was not class. Anyhow, me 'n Foghorn Manganaro take Tommy on an outing to Ebbets Field where we stuff ourselves with peanuts, hot dogs and soda pop an' make Tommy feel very comfortable by seein' he screws up one night of his life at the Villa Vito but here are nine guys, our beloved Bums, who screw up almost every day of their lives. We watch them hand the game on a silver platter to the Pittsburgh Pirates by two men runnin' to the same base, droppin' pop flies, throwin' the ball to the wrong base – these guys did it all. An' during the whole nine innings the crowd is takin' off an' razzin' 'em like crazy, "Hey, Stengel, tell Frey his head is on backwards again", "Whadda bunch of Bums – youse guys belong in a circus, not a ballpark" but it is all done with the deepest kind of love an' affection guys like us c'n show. It is under such conditions I feel comfortable givin' Tommy some Dutch

Uncle advice. "You're jus' like the Brooklyn Dodgers right now, Tommy. You're still one o' the guys an' everybody's wit' ya. Ya just did a real funny thing an' everyone's gettin' a good laugh outta it. You know that, kid, don'cha?"

Tommy just shrugs an' wolfs down his hot dog, lookin' straight ahead at the field. "It's awright," he finally says. "It don't bother me none." He is lyin' through his teeth.

"But ya know what bothers me, Tommy?" I ask him, although it is not a question to which I am really expectin' an answer. "I think you are chasin' a skirt who is quite unworthy of you." He swings around, lookin' at me wild-eyed an' I realize maybe I said the wrong thing. "I will allow no one to say bad things about my Rosie. She is some day going to be my wife." I decide I must summon up the courage to continue even though I know it could result in a total alteration of my face as well as other sundry parts of my anatomy. "Big Nose Sallie has made it plain to all that he will arrange Rosie's betrothal and it will be to some swank dude of near royalty from a place other than Coney Island."

"Even Big Nose Sallie cannot interfere," Tommy explains, "Because our marriage has been prearranged in heaven."

"Your marriage was prearranged in heaven?", I question him, not quite sure we are on the same planet at this moment. "Just what makes you think that your marriage to Rosie or anyone else is so important that the Good Lord, whose name I do not wish to speak in vain, will take the time to arrange such an occurrence?"

"I have had visions and dreams many times of Rosie 'n me. It is unnatural that this would happen just by itself."

"That's it?", I inquire. "You have made me very confused. I do not know who I will be marrying now Mae West or Marlene Dietrich?"

"You are having fun at my expense," Tommy shoots back. How he guessed I will never know. "Everything I have said was confirmed by that great fortune teller, Madame Chardova. That was not coincidence. That was a vision from another place."

Hearin' this, Foghorn, who is sittin' on the other side of Tommy, shrivels up in his seat like he wants to disappear, an' if there was room I would not be indisposed to joinin' him. We both realize there is no way for us to now confess to Tommy our arrangement with the not too idealistic gypsy. Life is too precious to chance such an admission. So, I figure, maybe try another approach. "Tommy, the ocean is full of many fish. What is so very special about Rosie, not meanin' to insult her in any way, but just pointin' out that whatever qualities she has are shared by others, maybe more so?"

He looks at me in this very strange way, like maybe my marbles have rolled down the street. "First of all, I have no desire to marry a fish as I do not believe it could be a healthy relationship." Okay, I thought, it is a point well taken, although Tommy is not graspin' somethin' here. He continues, "And in my eyes Rosie has everything a guy could want. It is not just her astonishingly good looks, but the way she talks, the way she walks," (for those of you who don't know, she walks like a pigeon-toed giraffe), "the way she sits," (Frankie Furtado would certainly agree with that) "an' the way she chews her gum. Nobody in the whole wide world c'n crack chewin' gum the way my Rosie can. It drives me absolutely crazy with pride an' love." I know when I am soundly whipped. There are certain things in life you simply cannot argue with. Tommy loves what would drive most normal people insane. Rosie chewin' gum always reminded me of a cow with a mouthful of firecrackers. I am beginnin' to believe maybe it is a match made in heaven. Frenchy Bordagaray strikes out an' the game is over, which makes me very happy because now I can get on the BMT, rush home an' lock myself in my bedroom, somethin' very necessary for my sanity at this moment. Foghorn, I notice, is keeping a very good distance between himself and Tommy all the way back to Coney Island, where Tommy waves an' says, "Thanks fer a real good afternoon, fellas."

"Yeah, sure, Tommy, our pleasure," we echo, an' run away as fast as our feet can go.

ROUND 9

The Dwarf was not one to join in such frivolous activities as teasin' or name callin'. If you recall that little ditty, "Sticks and stones may break my bones, but names will never harm me", the Dwarf was without a question, the party of the first part. The Dwarf was at the Villa Vito that night. In fact, one of the busboys swears that when Tommy rams Squinty's car into the Mayor's there was almost a little crinkle at the corners of the Dwarf's mouth; it twitched a couple times but then it died. It was almost like discoverin' life on another planet. The Dwarf makes no mention at all of the entire incident except when it first happens, he bends down, puts his arm around Squinty's shoulder an' goes, "Tsk, tsk, they just don't make cars like they useta."

The time has come though where somethin' gotta be done. The kid's identity has taken on a complete new look which can definitely affect the Dwarf's investment in his future. The Dwarf thought it would all blow over in a few weeks – some good laughs, a few jokes an' that would be it. Only now it looked like the Cockie Doodie

Boy could grow into a legend, another Jack the Ripper. Except for a fighter, he'd rather have Jack the Ripper. So the Dwarf an' Big Nose Sallie have a sitdown powwow at the Club to discuss Tommy's future, which is completely in their hands. It has always been Sallie's intention to move the kid up the ladder into the big money fights, and who knows from there.

They are sitting at a small table in the back drinkin' espresso which is a very impressive thing for the Dwarf to do; it is like another person holdin' a thimble in his fist and drinkin' from it. Big Nose Sallie has made it known he would like to start paddin' the kid's record by setting him up with all the humptydumptys they could make arrangements with. "You are barkin' up the wrong tree," the Dwarf interrupts. "I am lookin' to start gettin' paid back, not puttin' more money into a comedian who is goin' nowhere on an express train."

"Paid back?" Sallie inquires. "When did we put money into the kid?"

"We? We didn't. I did." And the Dwarf removes a little note pad from his jacket pocket, licks his thumb which he then uses to riffle a couple of pages, and recites, "One second-hand monogrammed bathrobe from the Estate of Tevye Chernofsky, a very excellent purchase as the initials are perfect if you happen to be a prizefighter named Tommy Curcio; two pair of boxing trunks, boxing gloves, speed bag gloves, an antiseptically cleaned mouthpiece an' a twice scrubbed an' cleaned protective cup, all purchased at a "deadbeat" sale from Stillman's Gym from pugs who couldn't pay their locker fees; an' four turkeys which we sent one every Thanksgiving for the past four years to his parents; an' one completely brand new pair of boxin' shoes because the kid would not wear shoes from anyone else's feet. Total from my pocket which I know I will get back–sixty-four dollars and fifty cents. Not that it will send me to the poorhouse but business is business."

Big Nose Sallie is actin' like he has a very wise espresso cup because his eyes are not lookin' at the Dwarf but they are staring into the espresso cup like it knows the answer to everything an' he is slowly shakin' his head in the way when you are sayin' 'yes' only his face is sayin' 'no'. "Believe me, I am in no way disputin' either the accuracy or importance of such investment but didn't that money come from our punchboard play kitty? An' don't we give out turkeys to everyone in the neighborhood if they are of the proper persuasion?"

"Please, my good friend Salvatore, I am neither a bookkeeper or accountant; do not let trifling details enter into this discussion."

"Okay," Sallie says, wagging both his hands in surrender, "but I am saying the same thing you are–let us move the kid along and start makin' bucks–big bucks if we play our hand right."

"Movin' the kid along means buyin' him a record, gettin' him in there with a set-up an' every tomato can costs money. He ain't worth the investment," the Dwarf explains. "Right now this kid is a joke. He won't be a drawin' card no matter what we do for him."

"Whaddya mean 'he won't be a drawin' card'?" Sallie asks.

"A fighter gotta have some sorta magnetism, a way about him that makes the people wanna come out to see him. He gotta be an animal, have style, flash, what they call charisma."

"Tommy is a real popular kid," Sallie throws in, "More now than ever."

"He is a comedian, a joker. The people that wanna see that would sooner go to a vaudeville show than the fights." The Dwarf goes on, "C'n ya picture a fight crowd yellin' 'G'wan, kill him, Cockie Doodie Boy, kill him'. It don't have the right ring."

"So we start callin' him Tommy the Tiger or Killer Curcio," says Sallie.

"You can call him whatever you want; everyone else'll still call him Cockie Doodie Boy, because it fits his reputation an' no one'll pay to see him. Salvatore, do you have any idea how many people paid to see the Manassa Mauler, Jack Dempsey when he fought Luis Angel Firpo, the Wild Bull of the Pampas?" the Dwarf asks.

"I am not the World Almanac," Sallie answers, now somewhat unsettled.

"More than eighty thousand people paid to see a guy

none of them saw before, Firpo. But he had a name an'
a reputation that went together. Do you think that
instead of The Wild Bull of the Pampas, the newspaper
and radio guys called him The Contented Cow of the
Meadows even eighty people would've showed up? That's
how it would be with the Cockie Doodie Boy. No
customers no matter what kinda record we built for
him. His reputation is already made."

Big Nose Sallie takes a deep breath. He knows he
must remain very calm and make a logical point with
the Dwarf. He does not even understand why he is
makin' such an effort but there is somethin' about this
kid that tugs at him, an' he always dreamt about
someday havin' a winner instead of a string of tomato
cans. "This is a kid who listens, he follows instructions.
You tell him to do somethin', you only gotta tell him
once; that is a very rare quality. It would be a shame
to waste that and throw such a kid away."

The Dwarf leans close to Sallie and whispers softly,
"Who said anything about throwin' away. These are the
perfect qualities for what we do with the kid. We make
him the stepping stone, the obstacle for every fighter
in his division on their way to the top. We seed his record
with a bunch of phony, out-of-town wins to keep him
plausible an' keep the odds in line an' we clean up with
a good usable tomato can, one who listens and follows
orders. Perfetto?"

Sallie shakes his head in the negative. "Donato, I

cannot agree, this kid can make it to the top ten."

The Dwarf once again hurts his face; he smiles, "Sallie, I am a reasonable person. I do not expect everyone to agree with me. That is not important. All I ask is that you listen then do as I say, capish?" The discussion was finished.

Although Tommy never had any great aspirations as far as bein' a fighter, like I told ya, it was just the direction Big Nose Sallie pushed him in, he was developin' the feeling that he wanted to do good, if for no other reason than to make Rosie Big Nose Sallie proud of him. He knew so little about the sport when he started that when his coach at the Police Boys Club asked him how much he knew about the Marquis of Queensbury rules, Tommy answered, "I know a little, only what my mother taught me, you know, like eatin' wit' your fork in your right hand and your knife in the left hand an' you shouldn't slurp eatin' soup. I try but sometimes I just forget." At least his coach knew then he had his work cut out for him. But by followin' instructions, doin' what he's told an' keepin' his nose clean, Tommy comes a long way in his five years as an amateur and now professional fighter. I don't mean it looks like there's a title in his future – nothin' like that – I just mean for a kid who knows zilch about the fight game he is now a credible performer.

Once he turns pro Tommy no longer trains at the Police Boys Club; he picks a gym on Livonia Avenue in the Brownsville section just to get as far away from the Coney Island crowd as he can. It is a long trip an' a two-fare zone but to Tommy it is worth it not to have to take the constant riding and wisecracks that so far do not let up at all. Even bein' away from Rosie every day don't matter to him because she looks at him like he is the Keystone Kops an' Laurel an' Hardy all rolled into one. What bothers him most though is that she has now taken up a friendship with that rat fink Frankie Furtado but he tries not to think about this too much because he knows that nothin' can come between him an' Rosie. Anyhow when he lets himself slip and does think about it in the gym he finds it actually makes him a much better puncher.

It is not too long after Big Nose Sallie's talk with the Dwarf that he visits Tommy at the gym an' takes in his workout, after which he sits Tommy down an' begins teachin' him the facts of life, an' I do not mean the birds an' the bees—these facts of life deal more with the vultures an' the buzzards. "Kid, we are goin' outta town. You are gonna fight one of Squinty DiPalma's boys in Philly." Tommy, who has never been out of New York City, is a little nervous but still excited at the prospect even though he is not sure that Philadelphia is even in the United States. "That's good, Sallie. I am in the best shape o' my life. I know I'm gonna do real good—

ya got nothin' to worry about. But what's the weather like in Philly? What kinda clothes do I bring?"

"Kid, clothes are unimportant. Philly is right next door, almost like the Bronx. We will be there only overnight," Big Nose Sallie explains. "An' I know you're in real good shape, but you're gonna sort of take it easy in this one. We owe one to Squinty."

"Ya mean the car I bashed up?" Tommy asks guiltily.

"Naw, kid, that got nothin' to do wit' it. Forget that." Sallie is not lookin' at Tommy right now because he finds it a very hard thing to do. "Ya know, boxin's a business, like everything else. And in business ya gotta play it smart. A smart businessman prizefighter can be paid more for not winnin' than a dumb pug would make even if he wins. Ya understand what I'm sayin', kid?"

"I am pretty sure what you are saying is it would make everybody very happy if I do not win this fight."

Sallie enlightens him, "Not everybody, Tommy, only the people that count. An' you get a very nice piece of change for doin' your job well. How does that sound?"

"I don't know. I was hopin' that all the guys would be proud of me..."

"Tommy, not only will the guys be proud of you, they will be grateful and indebted to you. You will be sacrificin' yourself for the good of your friends. What nobler purpose could any human bein' achieve?" Sallie was so impressed with his own speech that he became all misty-eyed and had a lump in his throat.

Tommy shook his head, "Gee! When you put it that way how c'n a guy say 'no'?"

"Tommy," Sallie went on, "we will carve out a real career for you. You will win some, you will lose some, at the right time. We will teach you everything ya gotta know. When we move ya up to the big money guys, the main eventers, you'll be covered by us in the betting pool, too. You're gonna be okay, kid."

"An' what about Squinty's fighter?" Tommy asks. "He's maybe gonna be a champion someday?"

"Whattya talkin' about? It's only a four-rounder; it don't mean a thing." Sallie is having great difficulty makin' a point he really don't wanna make. "Like I said, we owe Squinty one. He'll make a few bucks makin' some small local bets, we even our score an' that's it. Hey, kid, anyone c'n be a champion as long as he c'n beat everyone else. So he'll ride high for a while, get his back slapped by jokers who don't count for spit, gets his picture in the papers too much – it is an invasion of his privacy – an' yeah, he makes money, so what? He winds up spendin' it all on every Tom, Dick 'n Harry that hangs on to him as he is always in the center of a crowd. An' what does he do for humanity? Nothin'– he is one selfish slob who is only livin' for his own glory an' to feed his own fat face. But a guy like you – you will be a more humble person who will make your money an' be able to salt it away. An' more important, you will have the satisfaction of knowin' that you have taken care of your friends, of the people who count an' you will be revered and honored as a truly warm, generous, giving person. How c'n bein' a champion compare to that, Tommy? I ask you."

Tommy is staring ahead but focusing on nothing as he shakes his head an' sighs, "I only hope I am worthy of bein' such a person. But I hope Rosie will understand all of this an' not think I am just another ordinary loser."

Big Nose Sallie is puzzled now. The thought that Tommy's past mopping up of Frankie Furtado coulda had anything to do with jealousy, love or anything remotely resembling that never even dawned on him. Sallie loved Rosie because she was his daughter but the thought that another human being of the male gender could have any sort of emotional craving for his flighty, scatterbrained offspring was totally inconceivable to him. In fact, he simply did not want to hear of such a thing. Sallie had this mindset that he was the one who would make all of Rosie's decisions including who she would someday marry. This was not a unanimously agreed upon scenario but in Sallie's mind it was not open to a vote anyhow. "What has Rosie got to do with this anyway?" he finally asks, not really wanting to hear the answer.

"As my wife-to-be it is only natural that I should want her to be proud rather than ashamed of me. And you, as my future father-in-law, are also much in my thoughts in that regard."

Chameleons the world over could, at that moment, have learned much from one, Salvatore Pignasale, who turns every color in the spectrum inside of five seconds. "Tommy," this comes out with much sputum and sputtering, "this is a most unrealistic and impossible occurrence and you should immediately vacate such thoughts from your mind."

"Even if I wanted to," Tommy explains, "which I do not, it is out of my hands."

"Whattya mean 'it is out of' your hands?"

"I mean it is prearranged," Tommy goes on. "There are powers in heaven that have made it known to me that Rosie and I were intended to be husband and wife. I knew it all along, but then I went to that world-renowned, eminent gypsy fortune teller, Madame Chardova. . .you heard of her, didn't you?"

Sallie's eyes are now rollin' like a slot machine with a busted mainspring an' he is wonderin' to himself if the kid could have taken too many head punches in the amateurs. "No, I do not know of her, Tommy. But I do know you are partially right—Rosie's future has been already arranged. It is in the books for her to marry someone from a far off place who is to be a substantial businessman."

"But ya just told me I was gonna be a businessman, Mr. Pignasale, so it probably all ties in together. Anyhow, there is nothing we c'n do to interfere when there are powers we are unable to contend with involved."

"Since when did I become Mr. Pignasale all of a sudden," Sallie's composure is coming together now, "To you I am always Sallie, you know that."

Tommy smiles, "For now—someday I will be calling you 'Pop.' "

Sallie does not flinch, "Time takes care of all things, Tommy. Who are we to say what the future holds! But one thing it holds for you is Philadelphia, the land of soft warm pretzels 'n mustard."

"An' my first professional loss." As Tommy says that, Sallie is thinkin' to himself—The birth of a Tomato Can.

The next morning Sallie carves two large nicks in his face while shavin' 'cause he cannot look at himself in the mirror.

ROUND 10

I lean back in my chair an' take a good, long stretch as I have been relatin' how Tommy Curcio becomes a Tomato Can until I am very dry in the throat and am wondering whether I have explained to everyone's satisfaction. When Goldie leans forward with her mascara runnin' down her cheek I am already assuming I may not be completely done. "Wow," she sniffles, "that poor kid sure didn't go in the direction he wanted to. Okay, so now I know how he becomes a Tomato Can, but what happens to him? Where is he now and how come the cat got the tongues of those two over there," she is pointing to the Dwarf and Big Nose Sallie, "soon as you mention Tommy Curcio's name?"

"You may as well tell the rest of it, Sonny," Vito prods and Mitzi nods her head in agreement.

"Okay, okay," I give in very easily, "but first just let me get somethin' to soothe my throat." I snap my finger an' the waiter bounces right over. "What happened to dessert?" I ask. "How about bringin' us some rum cake? We are sittin' around here just twiddlin' our thumbs."

"I have already brought the rum cake, sir. It is eaten and gone."

It is at this very moment that the Clown picks himself up an' heads for the men's room without sayin' a word. I no longer had to ask my next question but I felt it would be good exercise. "Who has eaten it and made it gone?"

The waiter gulped uneasily, "There were only two pieces of rum cake left because we had a very late crowd from Madison Square Garden and Luigi said to make certain to save those two pieces for you. When I bring them to the table you are very absorbed in conversation so the gentleman who has just left the table motions for me to leave the cake with him. Soon I look and the cake is gone."

"It must have been very good?" I noticed a slight tremor to my voice.

"Very good, sir, as always. Is there anything else that I can bring you?"

"Yes, but you would go to jail for a very long time. No, I am only making a joke. Just a large glass of water, please."

"He just didn't want ya to be bothered with food while you were talkin'," Goldie tried apologizin' for the Clown. "Go on, Sonny, so what happens to the kid?"

I take a long swallow from the glass of water that the waiter has very obediently brought to me, then say to Goldie, "It is understandable that you shed a tear

for what happens to Tommy's future but if you do not
wipe that mess off your face, your boyfriend's name will
sound more appropriate on you than on him." Goldie,
who is a real lady, takes out her compact mirror, a
kleenex which she daintily spits on and in a few hurried
strokes scrubs her face clean and I continue. "Although
it truly is sad for Tommy to be turned into a never-will-
be you find it is hard to be sorry for a guy who does
not seem to be sorry for himself."

I go on to explain how, at first, all the guys at the
club are feelin' real bad for Tommy. We all put ourselves
in his shoes and try to feel what it would be like puttin'
in five years in gyms an' fight clubs only to learn you're
gonna spend your life in a water tank. It is true this
feelin' may be compounded by some sort of guilt over
the razzin' we have given Tommy ever since the night
at the Villa Vito. It seems the only guy who does not
feel sorry for Tommy is Tommy himself. In fact he seems
to be more industrious and dedicated than ever. Watchin'
him work out you would think he was trainin' to fight
for the World Championship instead of the patty-cake
sessions the Dwarf is setting up for him.

While Tommy is workin' on becomin' the consummate
Tomato Can in the gym, numerous unholy alliances are
being formed outside the gym which are cause for much
grief an' consternation. First, there is this growing
friendship between Squinty DiPalma and the Dwarf
which causes some concern for many of the Dwarf's

associates who are worried that today's favor becomes tomorrow's 'What have ya done for me lately' an' soon ya have to keep a scorecard to see who owes whom what. Then there is this relationship between Rosie Big Nose Sallie and Frankie Footer which is about as likely a match-up as Ruby Keeler and Oliver Hardy. Although Tommy does not enjoy havin' Rosie crackin' her gum for someone else he does not wish to have his confidence shaken so he journeys to Madame Chardova for reassurance which the aging gypsy seer feels might be unwise not to give him. It is possible, she surmises, that Tommy might be under the impression that with her readings come a lifetime guarantee so, maybe rather than being reported to the Better Business Bureau she decides to let Tommy in on a secret—Frankie has been appointed as a guardian angel and look over Rosie to protect Tommy's interests. This makes a lot of sense to Tommy as it is something he wants to hear and also brings about some eye-blinkin' developments such as at our Labor Day Block Party where Rosie, who usually bounces around like a chicken without its head, dances almost every dance with Frankie and at intermissions sits on his lap with her arms wrapped around his neck. It is during one such intermission that every eye turns toward Tommy who, until now has spent the whole afternoon an' evening like a fighter in trainin'. He does not eat, drink, smoke, dance or walk; he just sits and watches the festivities until now when he walks across the street to where Rosie an' Frankie are sittin' an' it seems nobody is breathin' or movin', includin' Frankie who at this moment seems totally paralyzed. The only sound is that of Rosie poppin' her gum and Tommy's shoes cloppin' on the pavement. And then, just when everyone is expectin' to hear the snapping an' crackin' of bones, Tommy slaps a five spot into Frankie's quiverin' palm an' says to our disbelief, "After the party you buy Rosie a root beer float or somethin'. Show her a good time, unnerstan'?" I mean, after all, isn't that the way a guardian angel should be treated? So the Rosie/Frankie thing lives to see another day. The next and probably most personally distressing of all the unholy alliances was the one between Sonny (yeah, that's me) and Teresa Collucci which was the result of a flippant promise made in kindergarten that I was forced to honor by Mr. Collucci because over the ensuing years no one made a similar promise and the Collucci's feared for a life of spinsterhood for their nineteen year old daughter. I was given options, of course, but none of them included living. Then there is Benito Mussolini and Adolph Hitler. This, as far as almost everyone is concerned, is the unholiest of all unholy alliances. Big Nose Sallie's family is getting messages to him from Italy telling how the people realize they are being led by a buffoon and to all of us he is a source of embarrassment and irritation and the Dwarf was constantly grousing over the frustration of having an ocean separating him from Il Duce. One thing he does is to have all the walls of the Mermaid Social Athletic Club painted red, white and blue.

In spite of all this the Earth is still rotatin', gravity continues to work so none of us fall off our planet—in other words, life goes on. Not only does life go on but things are not too bad at all. We are all doin' pretty nicely as Tommy has become quite a meal ticket as well as an artist in his chosen field of endeavor—or, rather the field of endeavor chosen for him by the Dwarf. He takes much pride in his ability to lose well and puts in long hours practicing and learning things that probably no other fighter ever bothered with before. For instance, if you ever noticed, when Tommy climbs into the ring the first thing he does is walk around an' jiggle his feet like he is doin' a little tap dance. But what he is really doin' is searchin' for the softest spot in the ring; there is always one or two spots that have a little more padding than the rest of the ring. This is the spot where Tommy will eventually go down. An' what falls he takes. He has names for his trips to the canvas—the accordion, where he folds up an' goes down in sections; the pole-ax, where—Whomp!—he goes down like a felled tree; the swan dive, which is very much like a half gainer off the three meter board; and, of course, the potato sack where he goes down just like you would push over a sack of potatoes. He has learned how to pull his punches like his arms have rubber bands instead of muscles. If you are thinkin' this is too much talent for one guy to possess, you are right. The Dwarf and Sallie have given Tommy many different identities. In Texas and California he has fought as Tomaso Corazon de Leon, the Lion-hearted kid from Chihuahua, Mexico. He was Indian Joe Tom-Tom in Butte, Montana and in Chicago and Miami he often fought as Herbie Feldman, with the Star of David on his trunks. He was whoever the people would pay the most to see, whether to win or get beat up because it was necessary that he should also win a good number of fights, especially under his real name; in fact he had many wins recorded without even havin' to fight. The results were just fed to the wire services by contacts of the Dwarf. He needed these wins in order to be in demand and remain a viable opponent. One day I asked Tommy why he worked so hard an' he says to me that Sallie once told him, "Who are we to say what the future holds!"

ROUND 11

In time, Tommy climbs the ladder to the big money fights. Even though he shows this strong work ethic, which, personally, I find very uncomfortable,—he is up at the crack of dawn each mornin' running the boardwalk then he spends all the rest of his wakin' hours in the gym—the Dwarf decides he must go to finishing school. So, on the recommendation of Squinty DiPalma, whose bets on Tommy's fights coulda paid for a dozen Auburns, the Dwarf brings in this sleazeball from Pittsburgh to train Tommy, Three-Finger Kowalski, who they say was the dirtiest fighter of his day and supposedly threw more fights than his much more honorable namesake, the great old Chicago Cubs pitcher, Three-Finger Brown, threw baseballs. The stage was bein' set for Tommy to lose all the fights money could buy.

Kowalski teaches Tommy every trick there is to pick up in this very strange art form. Instead of teachin' him how to slip 'n slide punches he would teach him how to ease into a punch; how to hang on in a clinch where no punches are bein' thrown an' shake your body to make it look like you're gettin' rattled by shots on the inside; all the different ways to hit the canvas convincingly which Tommy had already made into a work of art; an' how to grunt so that a pansy slap seems like a haymaker. I occasionally go down to the gym with Fats Suozzo and Foghorn Manganaro just outta curiosity. The first time I meet Three-Finger Kowalski I am somewhat taken by surprise. He looks a lot like Popeye, but after Bluto has given him one of his better goin's-over, he makes Foghorn sound like a soprano and much to my bewilderment, upon perusin' this gentleman's anatomy, I discover that he is endowed with five fingers on his right hand which is completely symmetrical with the distribution of appendages on his left hand. I therefore enquire of my good friend Tommy, during a respite in his workout, as to why his trainer is known to one and all as Three-Finger Kowalski. Tommy commences to explain that on occasion Kowalski may become embroiled in a confrontation with a somewhat antagonistic adversary at which time it is his modus operandi to swiftly and deftly insert the first two fingers of his right hand in such adversary's nostrils and pull forward, quickly neutralizing his foe and bringing hostilities to an immediate halt. It is at this precise moment that Mr. Kowalski's right hand is left with only three fully accessible fingers—thus the name Three-Finger Kowalski.

Big Nose Sallie is most unhappy at the Dwarf's introducing such an unwholesome character to the kid's educational program as he feels it is not only demeaning to the kid's integrity and innocence but also turns him into an actor or vaudevillian more than a fighter. Sallie does not know the reason why, but he still has a soft spot for Tommy, although he does not wish him for a son-in-law, and he realizes he may always regret never bein' able to know how far the kid might've gone without handcuffs. Now, I do not wish it to be presumed by anyone that I break bread with Sigmund Freud, but I cannot help but analyze that although on the outside, Tommy is a very satisfied and content individual, somewhere inside of him he has that very same regret as Big Nose Sallie.

Sallie makes his displeasure known to the Dwarf and lets him know that he feels quite capable of handlin' the kid himself without the services of what he considers a low-life spy from an enemy camp. But just as Sallie feared, the Dwarf and Squinty are now linked like Siamese twins, more out of distrust than respect, an' so the Dwarf just turns a deaf ear.

So just when it seems more likely than ever that Tommy is on a direct route to Nowheresville and Sallie has put all thoughts out of his mind of derailin' the train along comes a messenger of fate in the unmistakable guise of Tony Galento...Excuse me, Benito Mussolini. The New York World's Fair has come and the New York

World's Fair has gone; Hitler has been devourin' his way through Europe an' Mussolini has been pickin' up the crumbs, meanwhile, Tomaso Corazon de Leon-Joe Tom-Tom-Herbie Feldman-Tommy Curcio has been peddling himself all over the map and gaining the same kind of dubious fame and respect as those pictures that hang on post office walls, except they are usually in the Top Ten which Tommy is not. No matter, he is the darling of the Wise Guy betting set.

All along there is the hope an' the outside chance that Il Duce will pound a little too hard on his chest and thump himself to death but unfortunately this does not come to pass. Until now he had been hiding behind Hitler's skirts, occasionally stepping out to beat up on little countries like Ethiopia and Albania, but when Der Fuhrer's armies bring France to her knees and march into Paris, Mussolini heroically steps forward and declares, "I am on your side!" Although, like any redblooded American, I now hate Il Duce more than ever, in fact I think it is time for the Fuse to make him guest of honor at a dinner at the Villa Vito, I do not take it as a personal thing like it seems the Dwarf and Big Nose Sallie do. At this time the Club is not a very cheerful place to be an' we all try in our own way to bring the Dwarf and Sallie out of their respective funks which is caused by their shame over Mussolini. Vito, whose wisdom is highly regarded, consoles the Dwarf an' Sallie by tellin' them it is difficult enough to be responsible for our own actions; we cannot be expected to bear the burden for the sins of others and no one else's deeds reflect on you, not even your parents'. When neither the Dwarf or Big Nose Sallie respond in any way, Vito turns around an' facing the wall, says, "Okay, wall, thank you very much for hearing me out an' I only hope you will heed my advice." The wall also does not respond. Even the Clown, who has often voiced his belief that the only purpose the first five pages of a newspaper served was for wrapping fish, was much disconcerted over the effect world events were having on the Dwarf an' Sallie. On this one night he meanders into Chinatown after treating himself to canolli at Ferrarra's in Little Italy, and notices a number of the local citizenry wearing lapel buttons stating "I am Chinese," which he learns is so that they will not be mistaken for Japanese who at this time are becoming less and less popular with each passing day. Relating, in his mind, that the Dwarf's problem is of a similar nature, he procures one such button which, on the following day he brings to the Club and presents to the Dwarf. The Dwarf looks at the button then glares at the Clown, "What is this?"

The Clown answers, "It is a button."

"I know it is a button. I am not blind. What is it for?"

The Clown was acting now like an ice skater who thought the pond was frozen only to find the ice cracking all around him. "Being you are behaving at the present time like you are unhappy with who you are, I felt maybe you can wear this button so people will think you are some entirely different person."

Although most of us within earshot were very impressed that the Clown would wax so philosophically, the same appreciation was not shown by the Dwarf. "Joey, remove your button and yourself from the premises."

"You are acting in a most unappreciative manner, Donato," flaunts the Clown, much like the picador taunting the bull.

"In just one second, Joey, I will pound you so hard and so deep into the ground at your feet that when you emerge at the other end the button will be very appropriate for you to wear." The Clown, finally taking the hint, turns and leaves, muttering under his breath, "An' after I go outta my way an' spend fifteen cents on this. Can you believe anyone c'n be so ungrateful?" I do not know whether it is true or not but Fats Suozzo swears he sees the Clown wanderin' around for two nights lookin' for a Chinaman to sell his button to so he c'n at least break even.

At this point the Clown interrupts me, "I did better than break even. I was unable to sell the button then, but a year or so later I sell it for a big profit to a Japanese spy who wishes to travel incognito."

Goldie giggles and scolds him, "Joey, you will never go to heaven tellin' stories like that."

"That's okay, sugar. I'd rather go with you, anyhow, even if I gotta bring along an electric fan."

Gettin' back to how Mussolini opens up the road for Tommy a little bit...it is only a matter of time for something to motivate the Dwarf an' Big Nose Sallie back into action. That something is usually a number with a dollar sign in front of it, but this time the motivator is a living, breathing person who, in the eyes of the Dwarf and Big Nose Sallie, is the Anti-Mussolini, which is really not just a living, breathing person at all but a combination of Robin Hood, King Arthur and Jack, the kid who does a number on the Giant who lives at the top of the Beanstalk. Glowing reports are coming out of Italy, several other European countries and is even mentioned in the New York papers how Aldo Spoldino, the Italian champ knocks one, Gunther Schtunk, right out of his lederhosen to capture the European Welterweight Championship while the German's mind was probably much more concerned with his return to the North African front than anything Aldo was throwing at him. Of course, nothing was said about the fact that these were probably the only two guys in Europe still fighting with gloves. Nevertheless, Spoldino finds himself an immediate folk hero not just of the Italian people but of people all over the world who are against Hitler and Mussolini. After winning the championship Spoldino does not return to Italy but travels from Berlin, where the fight was held, to Lisbon, from where he lets it be known that he has no intention to return to Italy and fight in a war that he believes is wrong and states that Mussolini is making a terrible mistake joinin' forces with Germany. He also points out that his whipping of Gunther Schtunk further debunks Hitler's Super Race spiel.

For the Dwarf and Big Nose Sallie it is like they are in love again. Sallie walks around, bumping into things, his eyes are glazed and his mouth is set in a perpetual smile. The Dwarf, although his face is not made for smiles, does very cheerful things like shaking his head up an' down when someone says "Good Morning" an' when he is finished readin' his newspaper he actually asks if someone else would like it. It is important to them to show America that Mussolini and the Italian people travel in different directions, and they believe that through an Aldo Spoldino they can do just that. We all hold the Dwarf and Big Nose Sallie in the highest regard and treat them with the utmost respect because they have earned this with things they have done in the past but at this time we, each of us, keep inside the feeling that they may now be a little soft in the head. None of us would say this out loud because there would probably not be very many things we would say after that.

Big Nose Sallie is not one to let grass grow under his feet, especially when there is the Dwarf pushing him from behind. After trying through this person and

that person, finally, through his cousin Mario Pignasale
of Sorrento, he at last reaches Aldo Spoldino in Portugal.
Aldo's manager, it turns out is also from Sorrento and
is a neighbor and close friend of Mario's. Although he
too, does not have any great fondness for Benito
Mussolini, he has no burning desire to become a martyr
and therefore has returned to Italy after the fight rather
than join Spoldino in Portugal but is able and willing
to put Big Nose Sallie in touch with him. Whether Sallie
builds any big dreams or sand castles for him I do not
know but Spoldino, it seems, is overjoyed at the prospect
of coming to America and maybe even getting the
chance to fight for the World Championship. Who is
more overjoyed I am uncertain but I almost expected
to see Sallie and The Dwarf dancing the Tarantella.

They both agree that there should be no attempt
to book a fight against the champion, Fritzi Zivic. The
important thing is to glamorize Spoldino as a
swashbuckling crusader who is unafraid to stand up
against dictators and tyrants, a person who will wade
in with his fists flailing and a white-toothed smile upon
his handsome neapolitan face; someone who the
American public will relate to and wanna make them
stand up an' cheer him on while they sing "Stars and
Stripes Forever" and echo the chant of his fans in Italy,
"Forza Con Aldo"–"Strength With Aldo." This is not an
impossible dream that the Dwarf an' Sallie have–as long
as Spoldino wins–of which circumstance there is no

assurance if he is to fight Zivic who in no way will be compassionate to their plight nor is there any chance that the Champion's services are negotiable.

All of this means it is to be another day at the office with "business as usual" for one Tommy Curcio. When Tommy sits down with the Dwarf an' Big Nose Sallie in the back room of the Mermaid S.A.C. an' is told of this wonderful opportunity that awaits him, a chance to lose in a big main event fight at Madison Square Garden against a world-renowned contender, he expresses his growing unhappiness at being under the tutelage of Three-Finger Kowalski. In Tommy's mind bein' a Tomato Can was just doin' the right thing for your friends an' yourself an' following' the instructions of Big Nose Sallie, which was the natural order of things. It had nothin' to do with honesty or dishonesty. But in Kowalski's warped mind, which always seemed to run in reverse, if you were an on-the-level fighter who was engaged in a bout without a prearranged outcome then you were not giving the "inside crowd", of which Kowalski considered himself a charter member, the opportunity to invest their money on a sure thing which further meant such a fighter was a thief and a crook who was deprivin' poor, hard-workin' slobs like Kowalski from earnin' a honest buck. Just by Kowalski continually cursing and berating "unbuyable" fighters, Tommy was finding himself caught in a dilemma. If Kowalski said somethin' was bad, in Tommy's mind it hadda be good.

Tommy, who wishes very much to help his friends and himself, still does not want to be thought of as an immoral person so one day in the gym he poses this question to Kowalski, "Don't you think you are committing a crime against the person you are betting when you already know who the winner is going to be?"

"Don't act like the wrong end of a horse, Kid," Kowalski snaps angrily, "I don't need to know the winner of no fight when I bet. As long as I know the loser, that is enough for me."

So, as a result of this storm going on inside of Tommy's head, the Kid responds to "this wonderful opportunity" with an "I donno" which brings forth from the Dwarf a strong "I do know" and immediately converts Big Nose Sallie into The Great Mediator, "Let's hear what Tommy has to say", he calms the Dwarf down. "Tommy, what is it that is botherin' ya?"

But it is the Dwarf who answers. "What is botherin' him? I'll tell ya what is botherin' him. It is the old green-eyed monster that is botherin' him!"

"Three-Finger Kowalski has bluish-gray eyes; of this I am certain," Tommy means to correct him.

"What has Three-Finger Kowalski got to do with what we are discussin'?" Sallie asks.

"Bein' around him makes me into a most uncomfortable person and also causes me to ask myself whether I am leading a decent, purposeful life and unfortunately I am answering myself in the negative. Ya know, Mr. Pignasale. . ."

"Sallie," Big Nose Sallie interrupts, "I always tell ya I am Sallie to you, Tommy."

"I am sorry," Tommy continues, "Ya know, Sallie, sometimes I think I woulda been a happier an' a more respected person if I just woulda done the best I could—win or lose—like when I was in the amateurs. I cannot help thinkin' that is what is makin' it so much longer to wrap up my matrimony with your daughter Rosie—the fact that she is such a highly moral and good person makes it very difficult for her to have respect for a person of questionable character, which I am afraid I have become." If the Dwarf had the kind of eyelids that were able to blink, they would have at that moment, for the Dwarf is very puzzled. "Is there something that I do not know? Salvatore, do you possibly have two daughters named Rosie, one which you have kept hidden from me all these years?"

"Will ya stop it with Rosie, already!" Sallie is imploring. "Will the two of ya please stop it with Rosie!"

Tommy is almost apologetic now. "Do not think I am ungrateful for what you have done for me but I am very discontent being the person I am, and I no longer have the desire to continue my career as a prizefighter."

Big Nose Sallie is most remorseful at this moment and it is not because he is afraid the Spoldino fight may go out the window. It is because he is truly hurting for Tommy. He did not want to turn the Kid into a Tomato Can. He helped rob the Kid of any chance he had of finding out how good he could've been or how far he could've gone. He did not want to do it but he did it.

Tommy continues, "I know I don't have much education but maybe I could get a job like at Steeplechase or sell ice-cream on the beach. I don' wanna live by bettin' like some o' the guys do. I wouldn't feel good doin' that anymore, jus' like I wouldn't feel good fightin' anymore—that's because I ain't really fightin'. I am a fighter but I do not really fight. It is like somebody would be an actor or say they are an actor but they are never in a movie or in a show. How do you think they would feel?"

"You are coming close to answering your own question," the Dwarf is sensing an opening now. "It bothers you to think of yourself as a fighter who does not fight? Then think of yourself as an actor, being that you brought up so noble a profession. An actor, a fighter, what does it matter? They are names; they are labels and you can change them to suit your needs. So think of yourself as an actor and the ring as your stage; you are no longer a fighter who doesn't fight but you are an actor with a stage, and you are as good as they come, isn't that right, Salvatore?"

Sallie sits with a disconsolate look on his face and does not answer but Tommy interjects, "But I was not trained to be an actor. I was trained to be a fighter. You are just trying to confuse me with words but you should appreciate that this is a very difficult time for me right now."

The Dwarf realizes that he must now play his ace in the hole. "To turn your back on Sallie and me is one thing but to turn your back on your country together with the country of your ancestors, that must be a very difficult thing to do. I do not believe my sense of patriotism would permit me to act in such a way."

It was now Tommy's turn to be puzzled. "What has patriotism got to do with my being a fighter?" Along with Tommy's strong trademark sense of loyalty, honor and obedience, though somewhat distorted and misconceived, came the wraparound–patriotic fervor. Although we were not yet at war it was just a question of 'when', not 'whether' an' as tough as each of us thought we were, there wasn't one of us who didn't get a tingly scalp and watery eyes whenever we'd hear Kate Smith sing "God Bless America."

By the time the Dwarf is finished explainin' how buildin' up Aldo Spoldino is like sharpenin' the pin that we are going to stick in the big balloon, Mussolini, to let all the hot air out of, Tommy is gift-wrapped in a neat little package and tucked away in the Dwarf's hip pocket. An' I guess somewhere along the way, Big Nose Sallie is able to convince himself that the end justifies the means because he very efficiently goes about the business of makin' all the preparations for the big fight. He gets a room in the Half Moon Hotel on Surf Avenue for Spoldino, who is already crossin' the Atlantic and has got Madison Square Garden to agree to put on the fight although they are not thrilled to have Tommy Curcio as a main-eventer on such a big card. But the selling point is they are given the rights to Spoldino's next fight which very well may be for the title.

Squinty DiPalma is not exactly ecstatic when he is briefed by the Dwarf on what is to happen. "Bad business! Bad business," he snorts. "The wrong guy is in the tank. Who wantsa go on a short-ender? I gotta put up a Grand to make a C-note? It is plain an' out bad business. Ya got such a big head, Donato—I thought ya had room for a lot more brains!" It is only because they are tied together in so many give 'n take situations that Squinty is able to speak in such a fashion an' live to tell about it. Still, you can hear some sort of a growl comin' from the Dwarf's throat but he restrains himself an' says, "I explained to you, we are not doing this for money. There are things more important than money. I don't tell ya to bet; I don't tell you not to bet. I give ya the dope, which is keepin' my end of the bargain an' you do what ya wanna do. And Squinty, my friend, next time you say something funny about me like you are the Three Stooges, I just may be tempted to make you into three stooges." Squinty turns pale at the thought of the tearing of flesh and cracking of bones such a conversion would make. He smiles very weakly in bidding the Dwarf farewell.

ROUND 12

Aldo Spoldino's arrival is greeted with much fanfare by the entire neighborhood and he, in turn, loves Coney Island. He has never seen anything quite like it and is of the belief that all of America is like Coney Island – one big carnival. Immediately, Big Nose Sallie appoints Frankie Furtado as his guide and bodyguard which is one way of keepin' the little creep out of his home where he spends all his time droolin' over Rosie and Rosie, to Sallie's everlasting amazement, seems to enjoy such attention. His first two days in America, Aldo Spoldino learns to share Frankie 'Footer's' love of Steeplechase Park. Well, not the whole park, just the little auditorium where they spend the whole day sitting, watching as people enter the room over a small wooden bridge. As soon as they cross the bridge all the girls get poked in the backside by a clown with an electric prod while at the same time an air blower under the foot of the bridge causes their skirts to go sailing high in the air to the embarrassment of the unsuspecting victims and to the delight of many of those seated in the audience.

In no time this becomes Aldo Spoldino's favorite pastime, one he shares passionately with Frankie Furtado, who confesses to his new-found friend that he has applied for two years now for the position of the prod-wielding clown. Frankie Furtado has not changed, he has just grown a little bit. On Aldo's second day in America Sallie is looking high and low for him as he wishes to get him started in the gym but right now Aldo is enjoying himself too much to consider resuming training. When the Dwarf an' Sallie discover where he is spending his time, they are furious with him, but more so with Frankie because if the newspapers picked this up it would destroy the image they were hoping to project. Meanwhile, it seems Tommy was not looking to gain any advantage by Spoldino's absence from the gym as he chose not to spend much time in the gym either. This was the first time in his career that Tommy acted in such a manner but he felt it was meaningless anyhow and besides, he did not wish to be around Three-Finger Kowalski who the Dwarf insisted to keep on as his trainer.

It is just about now that Fats Suozzo gets his stomach scalded and his shirt stained. What happens is Fats loves to get to the Mermaid S.A.C. early on Monday mornings because that is when Vito brings in all the leftover pastries, cannoli and rum-cake from a big weekend at the Villa Vito. To Fats, this is Heaven right here on earth an' he is happily hummin' "Hut sut rawlsin on the rilarah..." as he approaches the espresso machine with a plateful of goodies in his hand. The only other person in the Club is the Dwarf, who often would spend the night there going over paper work. The Dwarf has already poured himself a cup of espresso and is still standing at the table when Fats gets there and gently sets down his plate before pouring his coffee. The Dwarf swallows his espresso in one mighty gulp, as was his habit, despite the fact that it was fresh and burning hot, at the same time opening the morning paper which is in his hand. What he sees on the back page stops the espresso somewhere in his esophagus, causes it to swing into reverse an' come shooting out of his nose and mouth full force like a geyser, making a direct hit on the protruding abdomen of poor, ever trusting Fats an' almost burned a hole in his new, white dress shirt. To this day Fats has this red scar on his belly to serve as a memorial for the picture on the back page of the Daily News showing Benito Mussolini, with a big smile on his face, hugging and embracing a seemingly equally glowing Aldo Spoldino, about to embark on his journey to America, with Il Duce encouraging him to return with the World Championship.

On the third day after Fats' unfortunate mishap, Big Nose Sallie sends him out to fetch Aldo and bring him back to the Club for a discussion. Fats goes straight to Aldo's room at the Half-Moon without going first to the Steeplechase Park auditorium as he knows it is pointless for Aldo to go there because he would not be able to see anything from eyes that are so swollen shut. Most of us assume that poor Aldo has some very strong allergy and when he is brought to the Club by Fats and almost climbs the wall when he hears the Dwarf's voice, without any medical training we have a very good idea just what he is allergic to. On this day the Dwarf is acting like one very calm, charming individual although he has already crunched two espresso cups in his hands. We are aware that he has had much coaching the past couple days from Big Nose Sallie who even forced him to read Dale Carnegie's book "How To Win Friends And Influence People". It takes much cajoling and many reassuring pats on the back to convince Spoldino that he is here just to talk and explain a few things. What the Dwarf and Sallie find out is that our hero, Aldo, has feet of clay. It seems that his big speech from Lisbon was motivated more from reluctance at being part of the Italian army than by a love of democracy and the free world. When Mussolini warns Spoldino that he will seize all his holdings, including his home, the bravado melts like gelati in the sun. Aldo returns to Rome where he meets with and apologizes to Mussolini who then permits him to go to New York, but as a goodwill ambassador for Il Duce now, on the outside chance he returns with a world title. Nothing that the Dwarf or Sallie says is enough to inspire the frightened Aldo Spoldino to stand up to Mussolini any longer. It is true that they do not threaten his life but it still seems to bother the Dwarf that Spoldino is frightened more of another person than of himself. They send a much relieved Spoldino back to his hotel where he is to rest before beginning training for the fight. As much as they would like to call the whole thing off now, it cannot be done as Madison Square Garden has already started beating the promotional drums for its big international fight, and the Dwarf and Sallie do not wish to be known as persona non grata, which can be construed as unreliable.

After Spoldino leaves the Dwarf stares at Big Nose Sallie and asks, "Can he do it?"

"Can who do what?"

"Can Tommy, this Cockie Doodie Boy of yours, stand a chance against a fighter like Spoldino?"

Sallie shakes his head, "I do not know, Donato. We have robbed the kid of everything he could have been. We have taken his future from him. But one thing I will tell you – this is one honorable young man and there is no one who will try harder."

"I do not want this bum Spoldino to win, Salvatore."

"You are taking too much upon yourself," Sallie warns. "You cannot change history with a prizefight. Spoldino is not Mussolini and we are taking this whole thing out of proportion. This fight is between Tommy Curcio and Aldo Spoldino, not between the Free World and the Axis."

The Dwarf nods, "A very pretty speech, Salvatore, and most convincing, but they probably made the same speech when David fought Goliath."

ROUND 13

It is true that every cloud has a silver lining and for Big Nose Sallie the silver lining was sitting down with Tommy and watching his eyes glisten as he tells him the fight is on the level and he'll be fighting to win. "Isn't that what ya always wanted, Tommy? A chance to maybe even fight for the championship?"

"I always wanted to give it my best and have people respect me as Tommy Curcio, not think of me as some dirty joke called the Cockie Doodie Boy," Tommy explains. "I don't know if I was ever meant to be anybody, but I wanted the chance to find out. Thank you, Mr. Pignasale, maybe now Rosie will think of me the right way again."

It is also unfortunately true that conversely, every silver lining must have its cloud. "Tommy, why doncha forget Rosie," Sallie was most uncomfortable now. "Because I am her father, I love her and I always will. But you have choices; there are many very lovely young ladies who may appreciate you much more than my Rosie is capable of."

Tommy smiles, "Do not be afraid to think of me as a son-in-law. I am just beginning to show the world what I am made of."

"Tommy," Sallie is speaking very somberly now, "Frankie has given Rosie a ring yesterday which means they are now engaged. The ring does not look like it has any more value than the ring you would grab riding on the merry-go-round but I think it is still the best thing she will get out of this engagement."

For a moment Tommy cannot utter a sound as he just sits with his mouth hanging open. Finally he forces this great big smile and croaks, "Don't worry, Pop, I always told ya me 'n Rosie was a match made in heaven. Soon as she sees it's the real me again ya c'n forget about Frankie an' his ring." In spite of the brave words Sallie couldn't help noticing as Tommy walked away there was no spring in his steps.

People express love in many different ways and there is often no explanation for tastes and desires but Rosie Big Nose Sallie held such a strong revulsion for Frankie Furtado that it was obvious why no one can understand how they can wind up as a pair. In Rosie's eyes he is shapeless, sloppy, unattractive and vulgar. I guess it is like sometimes you see someone so grossly misshapen or ugly that you try very hard not to look at that person but instead you cannot turn your eyes away; it is an unexplainable attraction. Also, her father's penchant to puke at the sight of Frankie was that much more

inducement for her to go after him, even though Rosie
enjoyed being the daughter of Salvatore Big Nose Sallie
as it made her feel special in a big shot sort of way.
And bein' a big shot she did not like to be indebted to
anyone or under any obligation. So, by going to Rosie's
defense and fighting for her honor years ago at P.S. 188,
Tommy actually coulda made Rosie feel most
uncomfortable, but instead she don't even know why
Tommy does what he does. Frankie's love of Rosie was
much easier to understand as he was coming out ahead
on every count an' Big Nose Sallie's dream of having
a son-in-law from Rego Park was going up in smoke.
But the real icing on the cake for Frankie, the thing
that truly made his heart abound with love for Rosie,
was the thought of all the inside tips he would be getting
now. He pictured himself lying in a hammock in the
backyard washing down giant hero sandwiches with ice
cold bottles of beer an' Rosie sitting dutifully at his feet
trimming his toenails. Right now Frankie was busy
borrowing whatever money he could get his hands on
because just the other day Rosie told him she overheard
her father saying that Tommy was going in the tank
again, this time for his new-found friend from Italy.

   As part of the Good Neighbor Policy, Squinty is again
called up from Philly to be told that the fight is now
on the level which makes him even unhappier than when
he was going to be covering a short-ender. "At least
before I was gonna make money. Who, in their right

mind is going to bet on an honest fight. I don't know what it is with you guys. I am better off giving my money to the Salvation Army. At least then I know I am gettin' a ticket to heaven."

Sallie smiles and says, "That is another bet you should not make."

Squinty decides that before absolutely backing off this fight he'll at least look at both guys work in the gym before going back to Philly so Big Nose Sallie notifies both camps that Squinty DiPalma will be comin' around for a look-see an' he asks Frankie Furtado to take him to both gyms, but makes absolutely certain not even to hint to Squinty that such a butterball may soon be part of the Pignasale family.

There is still one sticking point to this fight coming off and that is the crusading sports editor of the Daily Mirror, Stan Barker. For years Barker has been a thorn in the side of the Dwarf by taking potshots at Tommy Curcio's fights as he did with all fights that he felt had a little limburger mixed in. What Barker does not realize is that this is one time that the Dwarf couldn't care less if the fight was canceled. In fact he wold probably send Barker a Thank You note. A couple years ago Barker writes this column called, "Fights I Will Never Live To See" and right at the top of the list he puts "Herbie Feldman", which is Tommy's Miami nom d' plume, "versus Tommy Curcio...This fight can only be made possible by the assistance of the world's leading surgical team using the sharpest of scalpels to perform the most delicate of operations after which each fighter will still be only half the person he used to be." Barker was an artist making allegations and opening the public's eye to things without having any solid proof.

Barker has now decided to confront Tommy Curcio at his training gym in the hope of exposing him for what Barker is certain he is—a fraud. But Tommy, who is very unhappy working with Three-Finger Kowalski is working out on his own, which is a practice he is resorting to on an almost regular basis now. He is concentrating mostly on roadwork and calisthenics and is foregoing all ring work for the time being as that would put him under the watch of Kowalski. When Stan Barker arrives unannounced at the gym in search of Tommy, Kowalski is the only member of Tommy's crew that is present and he has received a call that Squinty DiPalma is heading for the gym. Kowalski has never met Squinty although DiPalma was the one who recommended him as Tommy's trainer so that is who he is expecting when Barker walks in. It is a very nasty mood that Kowalski is in as he feels his pockets are being picked by makin' this a legit fight. "Where's Curcio?", Barker snaps. He is a big bear of a man with a walrus mustach and thick-lens eyeglasses. Kowalski gives him the once-over an' thinks to himself, "No wonder they call a guy wit' shutters like that, Squinty."

"The kid ain't here, chief," Kowalski answers. "It is a pleasure to make your acquaintance."

Barker is not one to stand on ceremony. "This Curcio is as flagrant and audacious a performer as I've seen in all my years watching prize fights."

Kowalski is really miffed now—why should this punk kid get all the credit. "That is bullshit!" Kowalski roars. "This kid is Pollyanna. Anything fragrant and pugnacious about him is because o' me. Wouldja believe, he accuses me of cheatin' guys when I bet on the tank!"

"You mean to tell me Curcio does not go in the tank?", Barker shoots back.

"Only because I twist his arm. If it was up to that crybaby pussy all his fights would be on the level. An' those two runaways from a freak show—the Dwarf an' th' Big Nose—they are as bad as him now. How do you let them get away with such thievery—a fight like this bein' on the level. There is no money in such an event. I cannot tolerate such abnormal behavior."

Barker is forced to remove his shades because his eyes are buggin' out so far that they are hittin' up against his lens. He is a bit chagrined and taken aback but it is his story of a lifetime even if it does make him eat some humble pie. The real Squinty never shows up because on the way to the gym Frankie Furtado decides to make a stop an' show him the Steeplechase Park auditorium which, it turns out, Squinty loves as much as Frankie and Spoldino do so they decide to just stay there.

The next morning's Mirror has Stan Barker makin' a full column apology to Tommy Curcio and his managers while placing full blame for any past shady occurrences squarely upon one Three-Finger Kowalski and at the same time he gives his whole-hearted approval and blessing to the upcoming Spoldino-Curcio fight which is the sporting world's equivalent of the Good Housekeeping Seal of Approval. It was later that same day that Three-Finger Kowalski was packed and on a train headin' back to Pittsburgh with a one-way ticket. It was not known who, exactly, purchased the ticket for Kowalski but it was known that there were many volunteers.

Although Tommy was heavy of heart and no longer confident that heaven was still involved in his having any future with Rosie, he was more focused and intense in his workouts than he had ever been before. For the first time in his memory Tommy's life had a purpose and that purpose was to be the best person he was capable of being. If he was good enough he would beat Spoldino and no matter what, Spoldino would know he was in a fight but the one fight Tommy knew he had to win was his fight to, once and for all, knock out the Cockie Doodie Boy—get rid of him forever. An' if Rosie came along in that package—fine; if not it was her loss.

I always remember what my mother said when she made minestrone soup. She had a philosophy that when you had the right formula, when you knew your soup was perfect, that you had just the right stock—don't go crazy an' start throwin' extra this 'n extra that—stay with what you got, and my mother's minestrone soup was always perfetto. I guess it's pretty much the same as sayin' 'if it ain't broke, don't fix it' or 'leave well enough alone' but I like my mother's minestrone soup better.

It is a lesson that the Dwarf should have learned especially since no one will argue the fact that he is a very bright man. To make it more surprising, he is the one who always taught the rest of us to practice restraint. Anyhow, I believe it is a lesson the Dwarf did learn but chose to forget at this time. What I am telling you now does not go further than this table, understand?

It is just a few days before the fight and Big Nose Sallie comes out of the back room of the Club where he was talkin' with the Dwarf an' his face was whiter'n if he was a Grand Wizard of the Ku Klux Klan wearin' his sheet. What happened we find out later is that the Dwarf told Sallie he thought it over an' they could not let such an opportunity be passed up. With the odds at ten-to-one favoring Spoldino they would make a fortune if they bet on Tommy an' he won. "The Kid will try with all his heart and soul, Donato, but you know there is no guarantee," Sallie pleads.

"That's just it, Salvatore. There will be a guarantee. I will speak to Spoldino. We can offer him enough money to make him happy for the rest of his life. This is the big one, Salvatore," the Dwarf is breathing heavily now. "We will pool all the money we can raise. We'll even borrow from the Coney Island Italian-American Relief Fund."

"Donato," Sallie seems horrified now, "we swore we would never touch that money. It would be a sin. And what about Tommy? Don't you think we owe him something?"

"We'll count him in. He'll make plenty to soothe his conscience."

"He doesn't want money, Donato. In his mind he is fighting for something of much greater importance— his self-respect, which we took from him to begin with." Sallie does not realize he is shouting now. "Aren't you the one who's been telling everyone else that there are things more important than money?"

Donato tries to get the emotions out of the conversation by speaking very softly and calmly now, "Tommy does not have to know anything about this. He will fight; he will win and he will be a very happy, grateful person."

"He is not stupid," Sallie continues arguing. "He will find out and it will destroy him. Doesn't that bother you at all?"

The Dwarf answers very honestly, "No. There is too much at stake to think in such a way. I am not even gong to tell Squinty. I don't want any additional money bet on Tommy to bring down the odds."

"Donato, your honor. . ." Sallie is appalled.

"It does not involve honor because no one is getting hurt. As far as everyone else is concerned, the fight is on the level. Sallie, do not try to be my conscience. I will do the work, you just come along for the ride."

The following day the Dwarf met with Spoldino and the fix was in. He went along very willingly, partly out of greed, partly out of fear. And Sallie thought how differently this fight was turning out from how it was originally intended. It no longer was about glorifying an Italian hero or demeaning a dictator. It was strictly about making money at someone else's expense. But now that the decision was made Sallie knew he had to forget right and wrong and just be his usually efficient self and Tommy would have to learn that sometimes you have to go down much farther than you expected before you can climb up again—and there are times when you cannot climb up at all.

ROUND 14

I do not know why, but the week of the fight I have so many butterflies in my stomach, you would think I'm gonna be the guy in the ring, not Tommy. Right up to the night of the fight the Dwarf and Big Nose Sallie do not let anyone in on what is going on. Meanwhile, me an' a couple other guys like Fats an' Foghorn, we are hangin' aroun' with Tommy to try an' keep him relaxed an' loose, although the problem really seems to be that we need someone doing' the same thing for us. On Sunday of that week Tommy takes a light workout in the morning an' has the rest of the day off. We are very fortunate to have tickets to the Yankee-Dodger World Series game at Ebbets Field that afternoon to which we take Tommy as a way to keep his mind off the fight Friday night. This being a very historic occasion, as the Dodgers have never been in a World Series before, I am anticipatin' Tommy havin' a very enjoyable time but as the game is about to begin I see him cringin' in his seat mumblin' softly, "Somethin's gonna happen. Somethin's gonna happen..." I am about to say somethin' like, "Sure, somethin's gonna happen. Our Bums are gonna kick them fat cats all over the ball park" when I follow Tommy's eyes an' there I see Hizzoner, Mayor Fiorello LaGuardia throwin' out the first ball to start the game. I am picturin' in his mind that he is seein' all over again that night at the Villa Vito, him crunchin' the Mayor's car an' decapitatin' his statue. This was not the frame of mind I wanted to see him in. Throughout the game he stays curled up in that seat just waitin' for the roof to cave in an' continuin' with his occasional mumble of 'somethin's gonna happen' an' I keep reassurin' him, "Nothin's happenin', Tommy, baby." The game is comin' to its conclusion and I am much relieved that nothin' remotely resemblin' a catastrophe has occurred, in fact we are all quite overjoyed as the Bums are now closin' out the show with a big win an' evenin' the Series at two games apiece. As Hugh Casey throws his big curve ball past Tommy Henrich to end the game I give a big "Whoop!" an' pinch Tommy on the cheek, shouting, "Whadda game, hey, sweetheart! An' no roof fell on our heads, no stands collapsed . . ." I stop because Tommy does not move. His face is frozen an' he gives a gasp–in fact there is one whole gasp from the entire ball park which makes me turn quickly back to the field an' what I see I do not believe; the game that just a second ago was over and the Dodgers won was now not over because Casey's beautiful curve ball that ended it was supposed to wind up in Mickey Owen's mitt, but instead there is Owens chasing the ball which somehow did not wind up in his mitt and is now rolling merrily to the backstop while Henrich legs it to first base. It is then that the roof does fall in – at least on the Dodgers. Twenty minutes later we walk out of Ebbets Field like four zombies, all mumblin' to ourselves, but it is Tommy I am worried about, not the Dodgers or us. I turn to him, "Hey, so by a big coincidence somethin' very unexpected happened. Maybe it is even a jinx. It got nothin' to do with you." Tommy does not answer but he does seem to lighten up a bit an' we decide to take a cab home instead o' ridin' the subway especially since this first week in October is a real Indian summer.

By the next day Tommy seems pretty much back to normal, in fact he is one upbeat individual and as each day goes by he seems to be growing in confidence. I am very impressed watching his workouts. He is makin' the skip-rope an' speed bag sing songs an' his sparrin' partners are beginnin' to say things like in their minds he got a real chance o' pullin' the upset. By Friday morning there is more tension an' electricity in the air at Coney Island than there is salt water taffy in the boardwalk shops. As Tommy makes his way to the subway on Surf Avenue where he is catchin' the train into the city for his weigh-in and pre-fight nap, everything stops. The carny barkers stop barking, the vendors stop vending, it seems that the air stops movin'.

It starts very softly, like with one voice, "Good luck, Tommy", then another, "Go get 'im, Kid", an' before you know it a whole crowd is clappin' as he walks by an' cheerin' him on loudly and emotionally all the way to the subway. There are no smart alecky jokes or jeers, no teasing or taunting, only admiration and well-wishing. This is the treatment reserved for a proud championship prizefighter, not a Tomato Can. Me, Fats an' Foghorn went along with Tommy an' lucky thing I had some kleenex in my pocket because four noses hadda be blown out, but good.

The Dwarf an' Big Nose Sallie had been very conspicuous by their bein' no where aroun' most of the week. They are caught up in the excitement too but for a most different reason. This is the night their number is comin' in an' it is turnin' out so simple it is almost ridiculous. The Dwarf bet everything he could beg, borrow or steal on this one. They cleaned out the Coney Island Italian-American Relief Fund, but it was only a loan. Every last cent would be repaid an' they would walk away with all the money they would ever need. They stayed away from everyone until fight night because they did not want to take any chance of revealin' what was to happen. They spoke to no one, at least not while they were awake.

It seems Big Nose Sallie has this little problem, sort of a combination of insomnia, the heebie-jeebies and conscienitis. What happens is because he does not always follow his own good advice when he is awake, he starts arguin' with himself when he goes to bed, an' his conscience starts lecturin' the rest of him which does not make for a very restful night's sleep as he is busy blabbin' away, an' if he should completely wake up in the middle of such an argument, then he gets the heebie jeebies. The situation that is now occurring is extremely distressing to him because it involves cheating, a bit of backstabbing of friends and most of all, the breaking of such an important promise to Tommy. Well, the night before the fight Rosie Big Nose Sallie, who has been out a bit later than the house rules allow, is tip-toein' past her father's bedroom just when he is in the middle of receiving this terrific tongue-lashing from himself, an' also the Dwarf, who is not even there is bein' given a 'what's for'. Ordinarily Rosie couldn't care less about such matters as prize fights an' bettin an' tank jobs but she has become much intrigued at what has been happening with Tommy Curcio lately and is beginnin' to maybe have some second thoughts, so she stops for a moment when she hears his name come up in this nocturnal soliloquy. "Go ahead, just lay there, Mr. Innocence," her father is shouting at himself, "an' the same goes for you, Donato; you know that by havin' this Spoldino go in the tank you are breaking a sacred promise to Tommy." Rosie shrugged and went on to her room. She couldn't understand what was so terrible makin' sure Tommy would win, especially since it was probably the only way he could possibly win, anyhow.

When we get to the Garden it is quite early but the outer lobby is already crowded an' many of the insiders an' big guys are millin' around although there is not much real bettin' on a ten-to-one fight. There is more sentiment than financial backing for Tommy. Nedick's is so packed, you cannot get close to the hot dog counter, which I gotta admit, greatly dismays me even though my stomach is now doin' flip-flops. As the crowd starts movin' into the inner lobby there is suddenly a big hubbub an' commotion and the gendarmes start makin' a path from Eighth Avenue right into the Garden through which they are leading the Mayor of New York. Tommy, who has been a model of cool confidence all through the day, looks like he is going to crack up worse than Humpty-Dumpty ever did, and to make matters worse as they are wisking LaGuardia through, he skids to a halt right in front of Tommy, looks the Kid square in the face an' asks him, "Don't I know you, young man?" He might as well have been speakin' to a Franciscan monk for all the chance there was that Tommy would answer him. One of the cops whispers in the Mayor's ear, "That's Tommy Curcio. He's fightin' Spoldino, the Eyetalian champ in the main event."

For a moment the Mayor seems in deep thought. "Hmmm, it just seems to me that we've met somewhere." Then, bursting into a full smile, "Oh, well. It must be from your picture on the posters. Good luck, Curcio, you know, for the old Red, White and Blue." As the Mayor continues into the Garden Tommy stands there in a cold-sweated daze. I know I gotta snap him out of it so I give him a good shake an' tell him, "Forget it, Kid. It don't mean a thing. See, he don't even know you no more."

Tommy gives me one of those "we'll see" smiles. "It is a foreboding, Sonny, you'll see. It is a foreboding."

I give him my look of surrender an' go, "Yeah, I know, Tommy—Somethin's gonna happen. Somethin's gonna happen."

What neither of us could know is that somethin' already is happenin'. After Big Nose Sallie leaves for the Club to meet the Dwarf an' go to the Garden together, Rosie decides to spruce up an' go to the fight with Frankie especially since it seems now everyone is suddenly interested in Tommy Curcio. It is not too long before Frankie Footer comes struttin' in whistlin' a happy tune which makes Rosie think of the Seven Dwarfs only she is not sure which one. She is about to settle on Dopey but she decides he is too cute. "What are you so happy about?" 'Happy', she thinks—no, that is not the right Dwarf either.

"And what is there not to be happy about?", Frankie beams, "especially when I am about to come into enough extra cabbage so that I can buy a new Stromberg-Carlson."

"Whatja do, clean out under the cushions in the lobby of the Half-Moon Hotel again?"

"Very funny. I hear they will be lookin' for a replacement for Fannie Brice pretty soon." Then Frankie continues, "I am talkin' real money. I have gathered together almost two hundred dollars which I have bet on tonight's fight."

"An' where did you get two hundred dollars?", Rosie smirks, crackin' her gum.

"I borrowed it from my grandmother of whose eye I happen to be the apple of. An' then I bet her her own money at even odds because she cannot read an' when I read to her it is in sort of a digest form."

"How dumb can you be?", Rosie gasps. "If you bet anyone on the outside at ten-to-one you make two Grand, instead of fleecin' your own grandmother for two hundred of her own dollars."

"What are you talkin' about," Frankie is beginning to panic now, "I gotta give ten-to-one on Spoldino, not get. Leave it to a dame to screw up numbers."

"Why are you bettin on Spoldino? Don't you know?"

It looks at this moment like Frankie is suffering from apoplexy. "Don't I know what? I am betting on Spoldino because you told me your father said Tommy was goin' in the tank!"

"That was then; this is now. It is Spoldino who is going in the tank," Rosie blurts out.

"You are only kidding me," Frankie is praying. "You are being Fannie Brice again."

"What are ya worryin' about. It is your own grandmother. Just tell her it was a mistake an' call off the bet with her an' bet on Tommy with someone else."

"I can't. She's holdin' the money," he explains.

"I thought she loves you an' you are the apple of her eye?" Rosie asks.

"Yeah, that's exactly how it is. But she don't trust me. In fact she is holdin' my bankbook with my confirmation money in case I lose. Look what a mess you an' your big shot father got me into," Frankie is wailing now.

"My father was right," Rosie screams. "You are nothing but a perverted, cheapskate butterball an' it's only too bad Tommy didn't do a better job on you." With that she rips off her engagement ring and flings it at Frankie, hitting him square in the face. "Consider our engagement broken an' go shove your ring back up the merry-go-round where ya probably got it from."

Frankie rubs his cheek an' says, "A temper like that will someday land you in a lot of trouble." With that he grabs her and pulls her screaming into the bathroom and manages to get hold of a hammer and some nails that are on the foyer table and nail the door tightly shut, locking the shrieking Rosie in while he makes a mad dash down the stairs, to the subway, hoping to get to the Garden in time.

ROUND 15

It is nitty-gritty time an' Tommy has put his jigsaw puzzle composure back together again. He seems determined and confident that when this evening is over he will be able to walk with his head held high but still I sense that look of doubt in his eyes like he cannot believe that somehow fate will not intervene an' hit him with a left hook—it is the one punch from the one opponent he is not prepared to defend against. Personally, I still do not fully comprehend why anyone works so hard to prove something that does not need to be proven. I guess it is just for himself that he must do it, which I also do not understand because I know that I do not have to prove anything to myself due to the fact that I like myself, which is relatively easy in my case, being a person who has no faults. So maybe if Tommy really liked himself all this would not be so important. An' then there is Rosie but I find it hard to believe that after all this time and with what has happened that he would still be tryin' to prove to her that Tommy Curcio is no Cockie Doodie Boy. But one thing is for sure, he is out to prove it and it is an obsession.

Tommy has worked up a good sweat shadow-boxing. There is a knock on the dressing room door and a voice pipes, "Main event, ten minutes." I give him a hug an' plant a kiss on his puss wishin' him good luck an' am about to head to my seat in the arena when the door bursts open an' a totally outta breath Frankie Furtado almost falls into the room gasping, "Tommy, Tommy, I gotta talk to you. . .alone. It is a matter of life an' death, Tommy." Being that I am a person with no faults I have certain attributes like bein' tactful, knowin' when to be discreet and mindin' my own business, no matter how much it hurts, so together with Fats Suozzo, Foghorn Manganaro an' Tommy's cornermen I depart the dressing room but I have this sinking feeling that I witnessed the beginning of Fate dispatching its left hook and in what more appropriate form can it come than in the personage of Frankie Furtado.

When Tommy climbs into the ring with all of Coney Island cheerin' for him, although his jaw is set in a grim, hard line, his face is without expression an' all the color he got from runnin' in the wind an' sun an' eatin' rare, bloody steaks is drained from him like he was kissed by Dracula. From under the glare of the ring lights he looks out at the crowd; I am sure he spots me an' the boys but he keeps turnin' an' then he stops when he locks eyes with someone across the aisle from us. At first I think it is Mayor Fiorello LaGuardia who is sitting in the very front row so he does not have to look over anyone's head which he physically cannot do, then I think it is the Dwarf an' Big Nose Sallie who are sittin' about four rows behind the Mayor an' then I realize that it is Squinty DiPalma who is sittin' in the aisle seat in the same row as theirs that Tommy is giving what looks like the evil eye, for what reason I do not know and obviously either does Squinty who gives a little smirk an' waves to Tommy acknowledging what he accepts as a greeting. I c'n almost swear I see Tommy bare his teeth like a rabid dog. What brings this on I cannot even guess but I must assume it has something to do with the little dressing room tete-a-tete.

As I related I generally do not pay for my tickets at Madison Square Garden as they are gifts for services rendered, but I very gladly would have paid any price of admission to have been able to stay in that dressing room a few minutes ago. What is pieced together in retrospect is that when we leave the dressing room Frankie blurts out, "Oh, God, Tommy, what a terrible thing. Squinty got her an' will stop at nothing to have things done his way!"

"Hold on. I don't know what you are talkin' about. Who has Squinty got an' what does he want done his way?"

"Tommy, you don't know the half of it," Frankie moans.

"I don't know the half of it?", Tommy questions. "I don't know none of it, an' if ya don't tell me right now I ain't gonna know because I gotta be out there in about two minutes."

Frankie is like John Barrymore as he grabs hold of the front of Tommy's robe an' cries, "Me 'n Rosie were just gettin' ready to leave for the Garden, all Rosie kept sayin' was 'I wanna see Tommy fight', 'I wanna see Tommy fight'—it seems like it was her only simple pleasure in life—I gotta admit, I'm only human, I was jealous over it—but sometimes ya gotta be a big person, anyhow, we are just about to leave when the front door is busted open an' there is Squinty DiPalma with a whole bunch of his henchmen an' all o' them includin' Squinty looked like they were crazy from opium or reefers—or even worse."

"Well, what'd he want?", Tommy was havin' a very difficult time swallowin' this but never had he seen such a convincing performance.

"He said, Tommy," Frankie was sniveling now, "that he was two-timed by the Dwarf. He says when the fight was first made the Dwarf tells him Spoldino is gonna win."

"I know that," Tommy concurs, "but that has changed because of his questionable attachment for Benito Mussolini."

"But Squinty says nobody checks with him. Meanwhile he bets everything he owns or can borrow on Spoldino. He says he even bets all his wealthy, bedridden grandmother's fortune on Spoldino. Can ya imagine anyone doin' such a thing?"

"But Spoldino ain't gonna win," Tommy assures him, "not if I have anything to do about it, which I do."

"So poor Rosie will pay the price," Frankie cries, "but that is the way she would want it. The very last thing that she said to me as Squinty's mobsters took her bound and blindfolded to their hideout with orders to kill her if Spoldino loses was, 'tell Tommy to win it in memory of me—let him not yield to a mobster's extortion. What is my life in comparison to what Tommy can accomplish?' "

Although the tears were now cascading down Tommy's face he could not help but still be skeptical. He could understand Rosie finally waking up to the truth—he always believed it would happen some day—but never to such a degree. "I can't believe you're lyin', but how do I know you're tellin' the truth?"

Frankie's eyes are downcast as he reaches into his pants pocket, an' takes out a small, brassy object, "I didn't want to cause you undue concern, but Squinty said in case things didn't work out an' they hadda exterminate Rosie he wanted Big Nose Sallie to have her personal belongings, for ol' times sake, so just as they are draggin' her out he pulls her engagement ring off her finger," at which point Frankie stifles a big boo-hoo sob, "an gives it to me for Sallie... just if...", an' he flips the ring over to Tommy who has no easy time catchin' it or holdin' it with boxing gloves on. As it is certainly a most distinctive sort of engagement ring there is no question in Tommy's mind that it is Rosie's. Also, there is no question that the fight that goes on in the ring cannot compare with the fight that is going on inside of Tommy right now. All the way from his dressing room to the ring the battle is going on inside Tommy's head and he was finally convinced that tonight he was fighting for himself, not for Rosie or the Red, White and Blue or for anyone—just for himself. In fact, he didn't think he could ever have feelings for anyone who could hook up with a Frankie Furtado.

ROUND 16

When the referee is finished giving his instructions in the center of the ring and the ring announcer says, "May the better man win", both Spoldino and Tommy shake their heads in the negative. It is probably the first fight in history where both fighters give it their best, all-out effort to lose.

For anyone who was at the Garden that night what they witness is something they can never forget, even if some try very hard. Also, no one ever asked for a rematch. Right at the opening bell Tommy bolts across the ring an' lets out all the frustration an' anger that's in him by bouncing a big, sweeping right hand square on Spoldino's ear. He musta heard telephones ringin' all over the world from that one. Spoldino falls right into a clinch, hissing in Tommy's ear, "Hey, you crazy — what-a you hit me so hard for? You donna gotta hurt me." Tommy, who has no idea that Aldo is in the tank cannot understand why he is talkin' like that except he must have a yellow streak, so he pushes him off and proceeds to bop him one with his left, right on the bridge of the nose. It is the kind of punch that makes you think you got a faucet in your eyes, so much water comes out of them. It is Tommy's intention that until he makes up his mind as to who gets sacrificed – him or Rosie – he will do the best he can to knock the stuffing out of this Spoldino, especially since he heard he was pallin' around with Frankie Footer. With this last punch Spoldino becomes very angry, "You a real wise-a guy," he snarls, "I'm-a gonna teach-a you a lesson" with which he seems to forget, or disregard, what he was supposed to be doin' an' comes stormin' at Tommy with both hands flailing. But Tommy is right there to meet him head-on an' I gotta hand it to him, he is givin' more than he is takin'. The two of them are throwin' punches an' drivin' each other from pillar to post while the crowd is on its feet goin' wild. Between rounds I look around to get the crowd's reaction an' they are applaudin' these two guys all through the sixty second rest period. I look at Squinty who is havin' a grand ol' time smilin' an' laughin', really enjoyin' what he is seein' because he got nothin' ridin' on it. Just a few seats in from Squinty are the Dwarf an' Big Nose Sallie. I am sure it is them even though, somehow the Dwarf looks like a much more diminutive person than I have ever seen him look like before, an' Sallie is wearin' this strange sort of peaceful smile on his face.

The second round, if anything, is better than the first an' it sounds like Madison Square Garden is gonna have to cave in from the bedlam. After the second round I notice Spoldino is lookin' over at the Dwarf who is glowerin' at him an' as I am watching it seems the Dwarf is growin' back to full size again an' now it looks like it is Spoldino who is shrinkin'. There is sort of a sense as the bell rings for the third round that somethin' is gonna happen now; maybe it is because two human beings cannot be expected to go at such a furious pace for this long. What happens is that Spoldino stops fightin' like all at once his gas tank runs to empty but Tommy keeps comin' after him an' Pop!—he lands a left hand of not such great power high on Spoldino's head an' suddenly Aldo is sprawled out on the canvas at Tommy's feet, which immediately brings Tommy back to reality an' he recognizes he must do everything in his power to save a human life, in fact the defense of this particular human life seemed to be a full-time job for him. So, with the referee tryin' to point him to a neutral corner so he c'n pick up the count, Tommy, instead bends down, grabs Spoldino under the armpits and hoists him to his feet in front of a stupefied referee. There are now two-thirds of the people in the ring that are stupefied, and I do not know which one more so, the referee or Spoldino, an' about thirteen thousand more outside of the ring. As Tommy strains to stand Spoldino back on his feet he says loud enough for all around him to hear, "Excuse me for accidentally trippin' you, Aldo." The referee, who finally recaptures the power to verbalize shouts at Tommy, "What are you doing? You can't do that!"

"I accidentally tripped him," Tommy explains, turning towards the referee, "which caused him to fall down, so I apologized and assisted him to his feet as it was the only proper thing to do."

"Whatsa matter with you," the referee screams at him, "you hit him with a clean punch an' knocked him down." Tommy shakes his head at the referee, "Obviously, you were lookin' from a very poor angle. Now I must resume fightin' so please do not distract me." From the corner of my eye I see the Dwarf is now turning purple which is a very frightening sight, more even to others than to myself an' I think in a burst of creative inspiration which fortunately leaves me as quickly as it comes upon me—"I thought that I should never see a purple man the size of a tree."

The Dwarf's rage is most visible to Spoldino, who sits, quakin' in his corner between rounds, shruggin' his shoulders helplessly in his direction, like to say "It's not my fault."

From then on, everyone in the place is leanin' forward in their seats, rubbin' their eyes, not quite sure they could believe or understand what they were seein'. Tommy an' Spoldino were exhausting themselves tryin' to hold each other up. Each one was ready to dive to the canvas if anything even resembling a punch was thrown. Tommy's mind was made up—he had to save

Rosie. He could not live with himself if he turned his back on her now. Anyhow, to beat Spoldino would have no more meaning because it is obvious to Tommy that he is in the tank. Why he is in the tank Tommy cannot figure out but there is no question in his mind that it is so.

Meanwhile, there is this very strange kind of tension gripping the Garden because nobody really knows what's goin' on. Each person is waitin' for the guy next to him to jeer, boo or catcall because he doesn't wanna do it himself an' chance lookin' like a real jerk when he may really be watchin' one of the most strategic battles ever fought.

It is after the seventh round now an' Tommy is sittin' in his corner huffin' an' puffin', gaspin' to himself, "This guy is feelin' much heavier than he looks. I can't hold him up much longer." On the other side of the ring Spoldino is havin' wide-awake nightmares. He is picturin' himself in one of those carnival booths on Surf Avenue sittin' on top of a small wooden table which usually has six milk bottles on it an' there is the Dwarf throwin' these huge baseballs at him at about a thousand miles an hour. He is crying to himself why he didn't leave well enough alone an' go in the Italian Army.

But the Dwarf is just as desperate as Spoldino. Maybe even more desperate. The worst that can happen to Spoldino is death an' the Dwarf was beginnin' to realize that there are things out there much worse than death. If Tommy did not win he loses everything – more than everything, for he has borrowed more than he can ever hope to repay unless he wins. He sends a message to Aldo in his corner. It is simple, "Lose, if you know what is good for you." For Tommy, he blames everything on Big Nose Sallie. "I was like a father to that boy. How could he do this to family? Sallie, you are the one who spoiled him. Tell him it will be your fault if I have to kill him."

Sallie gets up an' turns to the Dwarf, "Donato, was he not a thing of beauty those first two rounds? Don't you understand, you already did kill him – five years ago." Sallie then turns an' walks over to us an' has Fats relay the Dwarf's message to Tommy, which he does an' Tommy answers him, "You tell the Dwarf I do not work for him any more. He lied to me. I must do what I must do an' he must do what he must do."

The eighth round starts with a substitute referee as it seems from what I am told the original referee was babbling incoherently between rounds and had to be taken to the Polyclinic for observation. Tommy was hoping that Aldo even touch him with a glove so he can go down, but both of them were being so cautious, they were circling each other keeping their hands hanging at their sides. It is while they are warily circling each other this way that Spoldino suddenly looks up above him and shouts at Tommy, "Watch out for the light!" Reflexively, Tommy cowers an' covers his head with both hands, or at least he starts to cover his head. As soon as he begins raising his hands, Spoldino virtually leaps at Tommy an' is able to bring his head in some sorta glancing contact with Tommy's right glove an' then immediately dives, I mean dives for that canvas head first. Tommy cannot believe anyone would resort to such lowlife tactics. He does not know what to do but he cannot let a human life slip away, not as long as he is able to breathe. The referee, knowing somethin' is outta whack but not knowin' what or what to do about it, begins counting over Spoldino. Tommy is now beside himself an' starts screamin' at Spoldino, "Ya dirty, rotten cheat. Get up or I'll knock your block off..." an' the referee is now at "five" an' the crowd is shoutin' their heads off, half for Tommy, the other half thinkin' he is a maniac, which he very well may be at this moment. He knows he cannot let the referee count to 'Ten'; Rosie cannot suffer such a fate! So, in an act of desperation he kicks Spoldino, but Aldo will not budge. The referee, who just says "Eight" yells at Tommy, "You can't do that. It's against the rules." But again out of desperation he kicks Spoldino, who again will not budge and the referee is now furious at Tommy, who now out of desperation and frustration spits down at Spoldino whose Latin temper is suddenly aroused an' he bounds to his feet with fire in his eyes an' at the same time there is a loud splintering crash as the Dwarf has just fallen over backwards and taken along with him his whole row of

chairs—with the people in them. An' Spoldino snarls
at Tommy, "Who you think you spit on? I'm-a gonna
teach-a you manners" an' he spits right back in Tommy's
face. The referee is now frantic, screamin' an' tryin' to
pry them apart as they are both in a frenzy, spitting,
kicking an' punching away at each other. And what is
goin' on in the ring carries over into the crowd which
is split in allegiance an' people are now so caught up
in the goings on in the ring that now all of Madison
Square Garden, it seems, has become a mecca of spitting
an' kicking an' hairpulling. There is no stopping Tommy
or Spoldino any longer as they seem to be in another
world, too carried away to even realize what they are
doin'. The referee is screamin', "Stop it! Stop it, I say.
Do you know how unhealthy it is what you are doin'?"
Then when they both turn around and spit at him he
can take no more an' roars, "That's it! You," pointing at
Tommy, "you are disqualified!" Then turning to Spoldino,
who gives one more good spit for good measure, "You
are disqualified, too. You are both disqualified for spittin'
an' kickin'. . .an' general unsanitary behavior."

ROUND 17

Back in his corner, with the Garden still in total chaos, Tommy is not quite sure what all this means, but then again, who does? He knows that he loses, which is good, but he also knows that Spoldino loses, which could be bad, so wanting to make sure that what he has done is not a wasted effort he does not bother even to wait for the ring announcer's verdict, but vaults over the ropes an' bee-lines straight for Squinty DiPalma who is in the midst of many jovial backslaps and gladhands. Before Squinty has the time to realize that Tommy is not here to replace his Auburn Boattail Speedster he catches what is probably the best punch Tommy has thrown all night right on the snoot which Tommy follows up by pointin' a glove-enclosed hand at Squinty who has been propelled right back into his seat an' shouts, "You are one cowardly, despicable gangster who preys on women an' children an' you are also a most unwholesome creep!"

"Yeah, dat may all be true," a now cringing, mystified Squinty responds, "but I do have redeeming qualities."

It is at this precise moment that Tommy sees Rosie Big Nose Sallie standing in the aisle crying on her father's shoulder, each sob being punctuated by the unmistakable cracking of her gum, as it seems some alert, public-spirited neighbors recognized that her screams was not shower-singing and eventually came to her rescue. "Rosie," Tommy calls, "you are safe an' sound!" He then turns back to Squinty, who has now regained his feet, if not his senses, "It is very fortunate that you did not welch on your agreement to set Rosie free." Rosie, whose eyes are very red and her nose very runny, has squeezed her way through the crowd and she is almost as surprised as Squinty at hearing such a pronouncement. "Whattya mean? Squinty had nothin' to do with it. It was my own ex-fiancee, Frankie who locked me up. Fortunately, it was in my own bathroom so I did not have to suffer any indignities."

It is suddenly very clear to Tommy that he has made a mistake of major proportions and that an immediate attempt at reconciliation should be made. So in an effort to rectify this monumental wrong he says to Squinty, "I guess I owe ya one" and holds out his right hand as an offer of apology, but Squinty is not thinkin' apology. He sees that right hand comin' towards him as another bop on the schnozzle an' remembers back to the Villa Vito an' is now convinced he is confronted by one first-class lunatic. There are certain simple adages that have made their way very comfortably into Squinty's code of ethics, one being 'discretion is the better part of valor' so he turns an' high-tails it for his life, headin' in the direction of the ring. Tommy, intent on convincing him of the seriousness of his apology immediately takes chase after him with the whole crowd whooping it up, not havin' the foggiest idea of what is goin' on an' from the balcony they are cheerin' with great glee, "Fight! Fight! Fight!"

Squinty is having much trouble getting through the milling crowd as is the Honorable Mayor, Fiorello LaGuardia who, it seems, has seen enough hooliganism for one evening and is trying to remove himself from his seat and the premises with his chauffeur/bodyguard Victor leading the way, but unfortunately Victor is no Bronco Nagurski and therefore they are pretty much stuck at the line of scrimmage just as Squinty DiPalma who is trying to cut around the aisle comes face-toface with Hizzoner whose eyes again begin to flash with distress signals of recognition. Before these signals make their final contact, Tommy, who is still making a gallant effort to extend his apology by racing full tilt after the panic-stricken Squinty, is unable to stop when finally coming upon him and winds up barreling into him, who in turn tumbles into the Mayor. This completes the final contact of distress signals to the brain and the Mayor becomes the second person on this night to have his memory jogged back to the events of the Villa Vito at which enlightenment the Mayor's eyes dart from

Squinty to Tommy, whereupon he exclaims, "It is the Maniac assassin again. And his assistant," pointing at Squinty. "I knew I have seen him before," he says, retreating at the sight of Tommy. "Victor! Get me out of here!" Maybe it is inspiration or maybe it is job security, but now Victor is very much like Bronco Nagurski as he cuts a path for the Mayor by smartly smashing his way like a battering ram through the Garden crowd and except for the fact that Fiorello LaGuardia did not have an oval ball in his grasp, the way that he zig-zagged through that throng, swinging out from behind the protection of his blocking back-chauffeur then side-stepping and eluding people all the way to Eighth Avenue, it would have been no wonder if some people had thought they were glimpsing the Galloping Ghost.

As the Mayor takes his leave of Madison Square Garden in this most unusual but rousing fashion, Rosie Big Nose Sallie manages to negotiate her way to Tommy's side an' I am busy removin' four more kleenexes from my pocket in anticipation of a very touchingly emotional union, when Rosie, true to form, cracks her gum an' bleats, "Oh, Tommy, why is it that you cannot rise to the occasion whenever a golden opportunity presents itself?" It is obvious that at this time Rosie, as well as just about everyone else, has no inkling that Frankie once again suckers Tommy. It is only Foghorn, Fats an' myself who have pieced this together from

Frankie's secretive pre-fight visit to Tommy's dressing room. There is no question that if Tommy speaks up an' chooses to explain the occurrence of these events, things may have turned out very differently but then again I do not know if Tommy really cared how things turn out at that time because he looks Rosie Big Nose Sallie in the eye with an expression that I do not interpret exactly as admiration or deep fondness and replies, "I rose to the occasion as I felt the occasion had to be risen to."

Meanwhile, another eye-poppin' happening is taking place just a few rows back – Big Nose Sallie is physically restraining the Dwarf, which we know is contrary to all the laws of physics. Not only does it seem that the Dwarf did not overly enjoy this event, but it is now obvious that he wishes to express his displeasure in certain very creative ways, all of which eventually necessitate the adornment of floral wreaths and black crepe. How Sallie achieves this feat of holdin' back the Dwarf we do not know – Fats is of the very strong opinion that Sallie must have to utter some magical word like "Shazam" but this is not a fact that any of us can substantiate – but it is with the performance of such an act that Tommy makes his way back to the dressing room with me, Fats an' the Foghorn formin' a flyin' wedge for him.

As soon as we get into the dressing room, we do not even have a chance to talk. The door opens an' Aldo

Spoldino comes bouncin' in an' I am almost expectin' festivities to recommence, but Aldo comes to Tommy with a big smile splittin' his face almost in half then, although Tommy did not get the embrace I expected he would from Rosie, he gets a real warm, sincere one from Spoldino who figured everything out in his mind this way, "Hey, you one helluva prize-a-fighta, Tommy. You know I am too big-a man to lose-a like-a dat – Dat's-a why you pick-a me up – you give-a me back the pride that Donato, he take away from me. Respetto. Respetto," an' he hugs Tommy again. As Tommy, who has passed up his shower to make a quick exit, which is a very wise decision in my mind, finishes puttin' on his clothes, Spoldino asks him, "Hey, you donna think you could-a beat me though, do you?"

Tommy shakes his head an' answers with a grin, "That's funny, I was gonna ask you the same question."

Spoldino laughs an' says, "Well, I guess we never find out then."

"We don't have to," Tommy says, "I know the answer. Tonight you did not stand a chance." It is then that the door opens again an' I am beginnin' to think maybe this is where you get the commuter train to Yonkers. But it is Big Nose Sallie an' I begin gettin' this sinkin' feelin' at the bottom of my gut because he is wearin' the Dwarf's face. Never before do I see Sallie where he has absolutely no expression an' there is not even the twitch of a nerve or muscle in his face. "You," he points to me, Fats an' Foghorn, "go home."

"Sallie," I know I gotta tell him what really happened, because it is now most clear that breakin' even was not good enough for the Dwarf an' him; they sure musta had a lotta bread ridin', "ya got to let me explain to ya . . ."

"I said 'Go home' ", he coulda spit ice cubes at me, the way he was talkin'.

I am not an argumentative type of person especially when it comes to a certain element of which Sallie is most indicative but I knew this was a situation that required extraordinary measures so I kept tryin', "Sallie, please, ya gotta understan' what Tommy did an' why . . ." If he cut me off with a bullet it couldn't have been deadlier than his voice, "It don't matter no more. Now go home an' forget what ya saw tonight." I have never been compared to Sergeant York, so together with Fats an' Foghorn, I turn an' go out the door; Sallie turns to Tommy, "You, come with me", then to Spoldino, "You, too, come with me." Tommy says in a choked voice, "Lemme get my bag." Sallie answers, "Leave it. Ya don't need nothin', just walk in front of me." An' that, my friends, is the last we see of Tommy. I lean back an' take a big swallow of water.

ROUND 18

Goldie's mouth is hangin' open so wide, it is completely blockin' the view of her cleavage. "That's it?," she finally inquires, "you mean that is it?"

I don't know if I am really a bit miffed but I act it, "Would you have preferred a fabrication? You wanted to know about Tommy Curcio, I told you about Tommy Curcio. You wanted to know about the Cockie Doodie Boy, I told you about the Cockie Doodie Boy. You wanted to know what a Tomato Can is, I told ya what a Tomato Can is. There are no final exams nor do I giva a diploma. If you do not wish to sign up for my next class, then do not."

"Do not play so high an' mighty to me, Mr. Accomplice-To-A-Crime," her eyes are flashin' sparks now, an' I am almost envyin' the Clown because Goldie has more movements and motions than a Rube Goldberg thingamajig, "how do you live with yourself for six years, knowin' what those two, drinkin' cappucino back there, which I hope is laced with arsenic, did?"

"Maybe it is because I don't know."

"An' I'm sure you went to the ends of the earth to find out, didn't ya?" she snaps.

"Hey, I'm really upset to hear this too, Goldie," Mitzi joins in, "but ya can't blame Sonny." ˉ

"Yeah, Goldie," the Clown pleads, maybe because he is a little guilty eating all my food, "Lay off a little, will ya, Sonny's okay."

"If you jellyfish are busy lookin' for your backbones," she carries on, ignoring everyone, "I'm going to see those two baboons. . ." and as she turns around towards their table she realizes she is bein' saved a walk because Big Nose Sallie is standin' right behind her without anyone at our table noticin' he was there or for how long. "Hello, Goldie," he smiles at her, "you visited our table before so now I feel it is only right that I return the visit, especially when sound carries so well in an almost empty restaurant an' I hear such a lively, animated discussion. Unfortunately, my friend Donato Langella does not share in my concern for protocol or the social graces. He is much more interested in his pastries and coffee."

"Oh, that is perfectly understandable," the Clown says with genuine approval.

"If it was up to me," Goldie goes on, "the two of you would be goin' to the electric chair."

"And if I was sitting at this table listening to Sonny's story I would probably share in your feeling," a smiling Sallie concurs.

"You mean it's not true?", Goldie asks skeptically, but somehow I am doin' a little squirmin' now.

"No. It is true. Even though I did not hear everything, I am sure that every word of it is true."

"Well, maybe you're not worried because you think you are going to take me to the East River like you musta done to Tommy an' Spumoni or whatever his name was, may their souls rest in everlasting peace," Goldie genuflects.

"It was the Atlantic Ocean," Big Nose Sallie corrects. Suddenly, everyone is inching forward, and there is a bit of suppressed gaspin', but only Goldie reacts. "If Sonny's story is true like you say it is then may I assume that what you have just said is a confession an' I can now make a citizen's arrest?"

"If that's what you must do," Sallie says, "why don't you bring in the Dwarf first? I promise you, I will wait." Obviously this is not the easiest of hurdles for Goldie to cross, so she very sensibly balks. It is at this point that Vito comes to her rescue. "Sallie, do not play games. If ya got somethin' to say, say it. Do not toy with us. Anyhow, just because we are the type of guys who do not interfere in other people's business, I now believe you owe us an explanation. We have been patient for a very long time, an' even though I have given my opinion that Tommy was a screw-up, he was still a good, likable kid, an' after hearin' certain things tonight I wanna hear a little more."

This causes Sallie, who always held Vito in the highest esteem, to change his mood; he no longer wiseguys us which is what he has been doin' up to now. He looks over at the Dwarf who is obviously not wanting to look in our direction, then turns his attention back to us. "Like I said, if I heard the story Sonny told you, I would probably feel like Goldie an' probably the rest of ya do, too. But, you know, a story ain't a story unless it has an end, and it does have an end and you did not hear it." We were the only ones left in the restaurant now. I am sure Angelina went home because the kitchen is closed and I am sure that Luigi's waiters are not putting us on their lists for Christmas presents. Sallie continues, "Sonny is a good boy. He knows the end. He is the only one beside myself, the Dwarf an' Rosie who knows the end, but like I said, Sonny is a good boy an' does not tell what he is not supposed to tell. But I think it is time to be told."

"Are you sayin' that Tommy is alive," even the Clown's curiosity is at a peak, "ya got him locked up in a cellar someplace for six years?"

Sallie, who is very cool, ignores the interruption. "No matter what you are thinking or believing at this moment, I am sure that we are all in agreement that Donato is a very wise person. That is why he is so respected."

"He is also a very large and scary person," Goldie adds, "and that is an even better reason why he is so respected."

Big Nose Sallie pays no attention to Goldie's remark and continues, "Everything he does is on a grand scale; his moods and actions run a range that we cannot even truly comprehend and frightens us. When he shows anger we hide ourselves as though from a storm but when he is forgiving or compassionate we all seek to bask in his glow. His kindness and generosity cannot be surpassed, but sorrowfully either can his greed. To be his enemy, one does not even think of such a possibility; to be his friend and be given the grace of his protection is to be blessed. And that is why his wisdom is so important, and whether we are aware of it or not, that is truly why we respect him. You see, it was his wisdom that held back his rage that night of the Spoldino fight, not my strength, for I do not possess that kind of strength. Our dreams are just that – dreams. Usually we never realize them. But on that night Donato's dream was to come true. There was no way it couldn't. Everything just fell into place. Yes, it was greed, monster greed, and he knew it and accepted it because at the end of the night he could spend his life on a tropical island and laugh at the world, if he chose. So when the impossible happens and everything caves in, even though he does not lose any money, to Donato, what he did not win was the same as losing."

"So it was his idea to kill Tommy?" Mitzi asks, horrified. "He really wanted Tommy killed?"

"Probably," Sallie answers. "I say probably because that is not the way Donato thinks. It is more like he wanted a world in which there was no longer a Tommy Curcio or an Aldo Spoldino. It did not matter why things happened or how things happened but that they were the cause of it happening. And if he had reached them we very possibly would have had a world without them. You can figure out by yourselves how that would occur. But again that is where his great wisdom comes in. It stops him just enough to permit him to have someone else carry out his actions."

Goldie smirks, "It took all of that for you to tell us that the Dwarf makes you do his dirty work. Do you happen to come in an abridged version?"

"You got me," Sallie acknowledges with a smile, "I do his dirty work. We each have our station in life or our job to perform. Mine is to carry out the Dwarf's orders. I cannot apologize for it, I was probably born into it, what Tommy would have said –'it was planned in heaven'. But when I do his work, if it happens to be what you call dirty work, there's no one who says I cannot clean it up a bit. I loved Tommy and it hurts very much that I let him know I did not want him for a son-in-law. I was wrong." Then Big Nose Sallie beams proudly, "And that is why I am so happy now that he is a member of my family." There are smiles all around the table an' many oohs and ahs an' Goldie sings out, "Ooh, he did marry Rosie, didn't he? Sure, that's why

you said Rosie knew about it besides you 'n the Dwarf
'n Sonny?"

"Yes," he answered simply, "he married Rosie."

"Oh," Goldie groans, "I got goose pimples runnin' all
up an' down my spine. Just feel 'em." For a split second
most of us were considering obliging but the Clown had
this look that sorta deterred us.

"Ya see," Sallie goes on, "I got this big family near
Sorrento and I do not wish to test Donato's anger to
see how far he would go. I have never seen him like
this before. So I told Tommy that night that I wanted
him to stay with my family for a while to give the Dwarf
a chance to calm down and get over this; he said what
ever I thought was right he would do. There was no
shame, I embraced him and kissed him. We expected
he would be there for three, four months. Who could've
known in less than two months we would be at war."

"You mean to say you shipped him off to Italy?", Vito
asks. "When did he get back?"

"He didn't. He loves it there. He has a family and
he became the person he always wanted to be."

"I don't understand," Vito says, quite puzzled at what
he is hearing an' I cannot say I blame him, "doesn't Rosie
live in Rego Park?"

"My daughter Rosie?", Sallie responds. "Sure, you
know that, Vito."

"But you just before said he an' Rosie were married,"
Vito continues. "That's how Goldie got her goose
pimples."

"That's right. I have these contacts an' I send him an' Spoldino over on a cargo ship an' in his letters to Sonny, who it seems he has corresponded with frequently, he tells him they become pretty good friends. When he gets to Sorrento, he moves in with my brother Gianni Pignasale who has a beautiful daughter named Rosalie, who is my niece, and who happens to like Tommy very much and vice versa, so Tommy becomes my nephew, which is maybe even better than being my son-in-law." What Sallie does not explain is that when Tommy first gets to Sorrento an' meets Sallie's relatives, he is immediately under the impression that Rosie Big Nose Sallie follows him over there because it is like they come from the very same cookie-cutter. But when he finds out how straight Rosalie's head is screwed on an' how she adores him because he reminds her of Errol Flynn, whom Tommy in no way resembles, he is head over heels in love with her. There was only one minor problem—he spends a great deal of time trying to teach Rosalie to crack chewin' gum like her flaky cousin, but it is an ability I guess ya gotta be born with. Everybody is astounded at this turn of events an' Goldie reveals that she now has a brand new flock of goose pimples, right over the old ones, only bigger an' better.

There is this great shadow cast over us now. The Dwarf has approached our table and is just standing there, listenin' somewhat sheepishly while Sallie continues to relate about Tommy's life in Italy then and now. Spoldino, who is himself a hero to his people tells tales of his encounter with Tommy, with much embellishment after which, if you were to add hot water to Tommy you would have an instant folk hero. Soon even Tommy starts believin' some of Spoldino's stories about him so he decides he better live the part. Along with Spoldino he joins the resistance an' the two of them become the darlings of the anti-Mussolini forces. He relates some stories to his comrades-in-arms of which he is somewhat misinformed. For instance, he tells them that Mussolini is the evil one of twin brothers; that his good twin lives in New Jersey under the name of Tony Galento. Many of them have heard of Tony Galento and they are amazed at this story—but if Tommy Curcio says so, then it is so. An' when Mussolini is captured by the resistance an' strung up in a public square it is not a pretty sight but there is the picture on the front page of all the papers an' at the time none of us even realize that right up front with their fists raised high are Tommy an' Aldo. And after that Italy joins forces with the Allies an' Tommy writes to me it is the happiest day of his life. I wrote back to him, it was the same for us over here.

"Hey," the Clown asks, "ain't that the day you cried, Donato?"

"Shaddap," the Dwarf snaps, "it was allergy." But there it is, a crease near the corner of his mouth. That is a smile.

"But," Goldie reminds, "the war is over two years now. How come Tommy doesn't come home, even for a visit?"

"First there are the twins," Sallie explains. They have two little boys that they name Salvatore an' Donato. Salvatore is a little bigger."

"Also," Sallie goes on, "Tommy is a very big person in Italy. He is what you would call a star."

"A star? What kind of star?", Goldie wants to know.

"A movie star," says Sallie. "After the war, which is almost three years now, Italy becomes the biggest movie-making country in all of Europe. It is the time of Rosselini, DeSica, and it turns out my brother Gianni, who has hands of gold, becomes a set maker. Tommy does not want to box any more, so he goes to work with his father-in-law. He does not last long building sets as the directors soon find out that he has this ability to fall down in any which way an' throw phony punches an' all those skills that he learned under Donato an' me so soon he becomes a stand-in and a stunt man an' he gets Aldo to do the same thing. Now they are the two best in the business."

"Once a Tomato Can, always a Tomato Can," Goldie groans. "It is such a wonderful thing – I mean, the poor guy deserved a break, but now it seems like he got the fortune Donato wanted."

The Dwarf shrugs, "It don' matter. I got my good looks."

"But tell me something," Goldie asks, "Why was it such a big secret and suddenly tonight it becomes okay to talk about."

Sallie shrugs, "Some things just take time. I told you, Donato is a person of great extremes, great passions, great changes. And I have much respect for his feelings, therefore I had to feel that he was ready to talk about it. We never even discussed between us, for months, how I handled Tommy and Spoldino, so how could it be discussed with others. When finally we spoke about it he was relieved to learn they were both alive and well."

"So how come tonight was different?" Goldie repeats.

With a smile, Sallie says, "Tonight, when LaMotta gets counted out sittin' on that bottom strand of rope, Donato turns to me and says 'Tommy Curcio could teach him plenty, huh, Salvatore'–then I know it is okay to tell the story."

"And what about your daughter, Rosie?" Mitzi asks.

"Well," Sallie says, "Soon after Tommy is on his way Rosie thinks she is now in love with him. Ya see, Rosie only loves what she can't have or shouldn't have. Anyhow, she goes to charm school an' she learns to crack her gum on the other side of her mouth. She meets an accountant from Rego Park an' they get married. I now have a son-in-law who can do my tax returns, if I were to report income, which some day I may consider doing."

"Are they very happy?", Goldie asks.

Sallie thinks a minute, then answers, "I guess so, but there is one minor problem. They have a den that he would like to use but can't because Rosie uses it as a sort of museum where she keeps all articles and memorabilia from or about Tommy as a fighter an' now an actor. It is like a shrine of sorts. Her husband would like it as a billiard room or game room, but Rosie says absolutely No."

"The only thing that bothers me," Mitzi says, "is that creep Frankie Furtado is probably laughin' up his sleeve for six years now an' nobody ever paid him back for what he pulled on Tommy."

"Hey, they want to close the restaurant, I think," Sallie says, watching the lights flickering. "You know, Donato has his car and driver here. It's a Fleetwood. How about a lift home, everybody?" At which Donato gives a wave of his hand towards the front entrance and in a moment the door opens and his driver saunters in with Donato's top-coat. "Come on, Frankie," Donato snaps, "Hurry up. It's late." It turns out Donato was not so generous with Frankie as Vito had been with Tommy. After the Dwarf figured out how much Frankie's little tale cost him that night, and as Frankie loves breathin' an' stuff like that, it was mutually agreed that Frankie work off his debt to the Dwarf until he is ninety-six, Frankie, that is. The question of the Dwarf going first was never discussed as it is so highly unlikely in the Dwarf's mind—an' nobody contradicts the Dwarf.

Frankie says things are really not so bad as he gets every Thursday off, unless of course, the weather is nice.

As everyone is most exhausted from the evening's activities, all parties other than myself gladly accept Donato's invitation. I explain that I am in need of some exercise and some fresh air after such a night and I choose to walk a while then take the subway. The truth is somehow it has a very uncomfortable ring to it – the Dwarf taking me for a ride!

I wave goodby an' I am surprised to discover that after spending the whole night in Angelina's I still have pains of hunger in my stomach, which is growling for attention. I sure hope the old lady has some leftovers in the fridge.

ABOUT THE AUTHOR

A born and bred Brooklynite, Ron Ross earned his B.A. at Brooklyn College where he majored in English and then studied for his Masters Degree at New York University after a two year hitch in the army. His desire to become a writer was temporarily side-tracked for thirty-five years while he carved out a career in real estate, not by choice, but rather as a fortunate pawn of fate. The subject matter of this, his first novel, is based on his peripheral involvement with the world of boxing where he had short flings as a boxer, manager and eventually, a promoter. As Ron explains, "All for the fun of it." But, today, when it comes to punching, he finds punching the keys of his typewriter much more satisfying.